Erin
THE FIRE GODDESS
LAVINIA URBAN

Erin the Fire Goddess: The Beginning

Text Copyright © 2011 Lavinia Urban

Disclaimer

This is a work of fiction. All characters and events portrayed in this novel as fictitious and are products of the author's imagination and any resemblance to actual events, or locales or persons, living or dead are entirely coincidental.

Cover by: Vin Hill   www.vinhill.co.uk

Edited by: Joyce Wetherbee

Acknowledgements

I would like to thank my family and friends for believing in me.

Dedication

This book is dedicated to my two beautiful little girls,
Erin and Kasey-Ray. Without you two I would not have
written this book with such great characters.

Chapter 1

Growing up is never easy.

I've always felt like an outsider. I've never fitted in anywhere. Even at home!

Yes, my parents and sister are great and love me whole-heartedly, but I still always feel like I don't belong. The three of them are outgoing, sporty and popular. People just gravitate towards them, whereas I feel like I have always repelled them.

At school, I am a loner and it's not necessarily by choice. Like I said, I repel people. So when my parents sat my sister and me down to tell us we were moving to their hometown of Galladale, I was kind of relieved, excited, nervous and scared. Even then I tried to hide the excitement I was feeling, it was just easier that way. I wasn't going to get my hopes up that I would actually make any friends.

"That's not fair!" My sister, Kasey-Ray's shrill cries of objection broke through my thoughts. I looked at my normally happy sister as she continued to rant.

"What about my friends? I'll never get to see them!"

She looked like she had been handed a death sentence. I could see the tears welling up in her eyes. Even when she was upset, she was beautiful, her perfectly proportioned features, long blonde hair and dazzling blue eyes.

"I'm sure they can come and visit." My Mum smiled reassuringly at my sister, after a quick glance of confirmation to our Dad.

"And besides, they'd only be a phone call away." My Dad added, as he looked at my Mum. It was a strange look, like they were communicating, without the need for words, which they did often.

My parents, Kate and John Tait, had known each other since birth. Apparently, my grandparents had been best friends and they had always known that my parents would be together. They used to tell my sister and me, that from birth, if they were separated they would cry. Luckily, both sets of my grandparents had lived next door to each other.

My parents were both born on the same day, only 4 minutes apart. My Mum is the prettiest woman alive, in my opinion. Jaw length brown hair, green eyes and an amazing smile. People often said she was Snow-White's twin sister. But to me, she was far more beautiful.

My Dad is just as good looking with dark hair, chocolate brown eyes and he can be so funny. Even in the lowest of my moods, he can always make me smile.

I sighed and stood up, ready to make my way out of the living room. Both of my parents turned to look at me. Kasey-Ray was oblivious to the shift of attention, too consumed in her own self-pity.

"Erin?" They chorused with puzzlement.

"I'm going to start packing."

My parents looked pleased that I wasn't going to argue with them.

I took the stairs two at a time and almost bounced into my bedroom. I could feel myself smiling. I fell backwards onto my bed and stared at the ceiling.

"Get a grip." I chastised myself. I wasn't going to allow myself to get excited. I sat up and turned towards the mirror, well if I hadn't stopped smiling before, I had now.

My brown shoulder length hair, hung there like rats tails, my green eyes had no sparkle and right there on the left side of my face, covering the whole cheek, was a huge reddy purple birthmark. This always brought me back to reality. I was a 14 year old freak!

***

We spent the rest of the week packing. I had already packed my room. Within two days I was ready to leave, so I decided to help Kasey-Ray, seeing as she spent most of her time complaining, and doing very little packing. The furniture remover's were coming on Friday and we were going to spend Friday night sleeping on the living room floor in sleeping bags.

The house looked so bare with all the furniture gone. I'd spent my whole life living in this house, but I didn't feel an ounce of disappointment. I doubted I would miss this place or the town.

Saturday morning, I woke to the sound of Kasey-Ray giggling and my parents trying to shush her. I looked up to see what was going on. Kasey-Ray was standing with her hands behind her back, trying to control her excitement.

What's going on? I wondered, as the excitement took over and she ran towards me.

"Happy Birthday!" she squealed, thrusting something small and square covered in purple wrapping paper. "Open mine first." She was almost bouncing, as she sat on the floor where I was still lying in an old green sleeping bag.

"Thanks," I blushed. I'd actually forgotten it was my fifteenth birthday. I sat up, shaking the present to my ear.

"It sounds like it's broken," I teased. Kasey-Ray rolled her eyes.

Slowly and carefully, I unwrapped the present, whilst watching my sister out of the corner of my eye;

she was trying to control her excitement. It was taking all of her will not to pull it from my hands and unwrap it herself. I took off the wrapping to reveal a small black velvet box.

"Open it, open it, open it!" Kasey-Ray squealed again, almost deafening me. Slowly, I opened the box to reveal the word sister, which was attached to a gold chain.

"Do you like it?" She asked without waiting for a reply. "I saved up my pocket money for that." Saving and Kasey-Ray were not usually words I would put in the same sentence.

"I really do." And I meant it. I took it from its box and handed it to Kasey-Ray, I turned around pulling my hair up, so she could put it on me. Smiling, I looked down, running my fingers over the lettering. Then I turned around to hug her tightly. "Thank you. I love it."

My Mum and Dad appeared, carrying two presents, covered in the same wrapping paper.

"Happy Birthday Sweetie!" They said in unison, as I pulled myself free of my sleeping bag.

"You get these two now." My Mum smiled.

"Then your other present when we get to our new home." My Dad beamed, as my Mum handed me the first present. You could tell it was clothing right away.

I opened this one a little quicker than I'd opened Kasey-Ray's, I nearly squealed when I saw the jumper I'd hinted at several weeks earlier. It was a long, sleeveless jumper, in a deep burgundy colour and I loved it. I quickly hugged my parents and was about to run off to try it on, when my Dad handed me my other present.

"The man in the shop said it's top of the range." He told me as I quickly tore off the wrapping, handing all the torn off paper to my Mum. I gasped when I saw what was under the wrapping.

"Wow, thanks!" I gasped, as I pulled an MP3 player from its box.

"We've already put some songs on it for you. I'm sure you can do the rest when we get to the new house."

My parents put an arm around each other and stood smiling at my delighted expression.

"There's a bacon sandwich on the side in the kitchen for when you're dressed." My Mum called after me, "We're just going to put the rest of our things in the car."

I quickly ate my sandwich, following it down with a glass of water. Rinsing my plate and glass, I placed them into the bag my Mum had left on the kitchen worktop. I picked up my rucksack, which contained my pyjamas and the top I'd worn yesterday. I was going to wear the same top today, that was, until I'd got my new jumper. I had also packed some sweets for the journey, along with my mobile phone and my new MP3 player.

My Mum had packed a couple of bags, full of sandwiches, fruit, crisps, and drinks, for the journey. I was the first to jump into my parents blue Volvo S60 and waited for the rest of my family to say their good-byes to the house.

When they finally appeared, it looked like my Mum and sister had been crying. I laid my head against the window, pressing my left cheek against the cool glass.

Kasey-Ray jumped into the back seat, dumping her rucksack on top of mine as she wiped away her tears. Normally I would have complained, but just this once I decided to leave it. Finally, my Dad pulled out of the drive and we headed off towards the start of our new lives.

It took about 4 hours to reach Galladale. We stopped once on the way for a bathroom break at one of the service stations. Both Kasey-Ray and I bought one of those little disposable tooth brushes from the vending machines. We spent about fifteen minutes pulling funny faces and taking pictures on our mobile phones, ignoring the strange stares from passers-by. Fifteen minutes was a bit much if you asked me, as the novelty wore off not long after I'd placed mine in my mouth, but Kasey-Ray did look hilarious.

Once we'd gotten back into the car, my Dad turned the volume up on the radio and we sang along to it. I wasn't sure if he'd turned it up to drown out our strangled cat noises, or so we could hear it better. When Mum pointed to the sign welcoming us to

Galladale, we all cheered and craned our necks to get a good look out of the windows. There wasn't much to see, apart from fields, trees, more fields, straggling sheep, a handful of cows, and even more fields.

My Dad pointed towards some trees, explaining that his parent's cottage was just down there. Both pairs of my grandparents had been deceased for at least five years now. I have vague memories of baking with one of my grandmother's and some other fragmented memories. The cottage had been in the family for centuries, passed down from generation to generation. It was left to my Dad when his parents died, but he had only been back to it a handful of times.

My Dad's parents had moved into the cottage a year after my Mum's parents had died in a car accident. It had been too painful for them living in the same house, which had been next door to my Mum's parents, especially when new neighbours had moved in. My parents had already moved away before my Mum's parents had died. She has always regretted not seeing them as much as she would have liked to.

My Dad's Nan was still alive then, and living in the cottage. She had offered them an escape from their old house and they had gone to live with her in the cottage. Apparently, she was suffering from bone cancer and didn't have long left to live; having my grandparents move in with her was a great comfort in her last days.

After a few moments we approached the High Street. There were a few shops, along with a bank, library, post office and a gym. Just after we'd passed the gym, we took a left turn into a small housing scheme. There were five housing schemes dotted around Galladale with a handful of farms, one primary school, a high school, and a community college.

We soon spotted our new house, the surprise given away by the removal van waiting outside. My Dad pulled into the drive and went to greet the removal men, whilst my Mum went to open the front door, Kasey-Ray hot on her heels, ready to lay claim to a bedroom.

I stepped through the front door into a long hallway; the stairs were situated in the middle, with a back door at the end. To the left was the living room, with freshly laid brown carpet, to the right a large kitchen/dining room. I walked to the kitchen window, to look at the back garden. It wasn't as big as the one at our old house, but it was big enough and backed onto a large farmer's field.

From upstairs I heard Kasey-Ray shouting, she'd found her room. What I hadn't realised was, my Dad had already been down to paint and carpet the rooms, he had given me the second largest bedroom, this being my final birthday present, knowing that if they hadn't Kasey-Ray would have claimed it for herself. Kasey-Ray's bedroom was painted baby pink and had a bubble-gum pink carpet, whereas mine had a purple carpet and pale lemon walls. Both my room and my parents were situated at the front of the house; Kasey-Ray's was at the back, along with the bathroom.

I slowly made my way into my room, I instantaneously loved it. One large bay window had a window seat that overlooked the front of the house and the driveway. There was a smaller window to the side. Placing my rucksack on the window seat, I looked out of the front window and saw my Dad helping the removal men who were starting to unload the furniture, whilst my Mum was unpacking the car. Kasey-Ray was already on her mobile phone, talking to her best friend, I knew she would be on it for at least an hour, so I decided I would go back downstairs to help my Mum unpack.

Chapter 2

Yesterday, my Mum had taken Kasey-Ray and I for a walk to show us the way to school. Before I knew it, Monday had arrived and with it brought the first day of school. I awoke feeling sick with nerves. I was up, dressed and ready to leave by 7:45am. School didn't even begin until 8:50am and it was only a twenty minute walk there, from my house. The nervous waiting around was excruciating. Rather than go downstairs to wait, I decided to go and sit on Kasey-Ray's bed and talk to her, whilst she finished getting ready. Kasey-Ray was actually really excited, which had made a nice change from all the crying and complaining she had done this past week.

On the walk to Galladale high school, Kasey-Ray was chattering on about all the new friends she would make and wondered out loud whether there would be any good looking guys here. I don't think she completely realised how people gravitated towards her and how most boys at our old school would have crawled over hot coals just to get a 'Hi' from her. She was a year younger than me, but could easily pass for 16, even at a stretch 18.

As we walked through the school gates, I noticed people had already stopped to stare at us. Kasey-Ray, caught up in the excitement, was oblivious to the shift of attention. I tried not to look around; I either looked at Kasey-Ray's face, or at my feet. I was kind of relieved when we stepped through the reception doors.

"Hi, I'm Kasey-Ray Tait and I'm starting here today." She told the receptionist in her most polite voice. "And this is my sister, Erin." The receptionist looked in my direction and seemed to stare at me in shock. She quickly looked back at Kasey-Ray, with a forced smile.

"If you would just take a seat the principal Mr Jenkins, will be with you shortly." Without a second glance at me, she quickly turned to the telephone behind her.

Kasey-Ray was still talking although I wasn't sure about what. I had tuned her out as we passed through the school gates; I just nodded here and there so she would think I was listening. I still felt sick. I should be used to people gawping at me, they always have, but it still didn't make me feel any better when people couldn't look at me without turning away.

"Kasey-Ray? Erin?" A tall, slim man wearing a tweed suit, with leather elbows and glasses that looked homemade, stepped through a door next to the reception desk.

He didn't look at me the way the receptionist had, which was a welcome relief. The receptionist had probably warned him on the phone, I told myself. He stretched out his arm and shook both of our hands.

"I am Mr Jenkins, The principal here. Let me be the first to welcome you both to Galladale High School." He paused to smile at us both in turn. Looking like he was waiting for one of us to say something, when we didn't he continued. "Well, if you would like to follow me, I will show you to your form rooms."

On the way, he explained what the school expected from its students, the times for lunch and other break.

He also told us that should we ever have any concerns, then we were not to hesitate going to see him. Kasey-Ray was the first to be shown to her form room. Before entering, she fiddled with her clothes and hair, asking if she looked okay, I told her she was perfect and she smiled widely as she followed Mr Jenkins into the room, where he proceeded to introduce her to the form teacher and in turn the rest of the class. All this time I hid out of sight behind the door-frame with my back to the wall until Mr Jenkins reappeared and closed the door behind him.

When we reached my form room, I stood hesitantly in the doorway, whilst Mr Jenkins introduced me. I heard a few people snigger when they saw me; some even craned their necks and moved their chairs so they could get a better look at the new girl, some making repulsed noises. I did my best not to make eye contact with anyone and I wished I'd tried harder. I felt someone at the table near the door looking at me, I looked around to see a red haired girl glaring at me with a look of pure hatred in her eyes which unsettled me and sent a shiver down my spine. Luckily, my form teacher called my name allowing me to break eye contact with the girl and her hate-filled glare. Ms Forrester was a short, stout, well-dressed woman, who gave me a warm smile.

"There are a couple of tables at the back, if you would like to go and take a seat," she pointed to the tables at the back of the classroom on the right hand side, one in front of the other. I decided to sit at the one furthest to the back.

At lunchtime I spotted Kasey-Ray sat at a table surrounded by most of her year who listened intently to every word she said. Smiling to myself, I decided to leave her be and go somewhere quiet to eat my lunch alone. As it wasn't raining, I decided it would be nice to go outside and find a nice quiet spot. I walked past other students, who quickly moved away from me to whisper to their friends.

"Have you seen her face?" I heard one girl ask.

"I couldn't exactly miss it," Her friend sniggered.

"It's like she fell out of the ugly tree and hit every branch on the way down," the first girl laughed. Fighting back the tears, I focused on the doors that led to my freedom. When I finally got outside, after what seemed the longest few paces I had ever walked, it took all my willpower to stop myself from walking across the schoolyard, through the school gates and all the way home.

Instead I found a spot at the far corner of the school field. I laid my coat on the ground and sat down on it, pulling out my packed lunch as I composed my thoughts. I sat staring at the contents for a good five minutes, my thoughts a blur, going over and over what had just happened. I picked up an orange and sat squeezing it in my hand.

"I wouldn't let them get to you." The voice startled me. Through the bushes a boy of about 17 stepped out. He had messy brown hair and the most amazing eyes I'd ever seen, like the colour of a blue-green ocean. I gasped, somewhere between shock and amazement. I don't think I had ever seen anyone so beautiful before.

He didn't smile though. He just looked at me with interest. To my amazement he didn't even seem to be repulsed by me, unlike nearly everyone else that morning.

He turned his head to the side and looked down at the orange in my hand, which I'd forgotten I was holding. I looked down at my hand and saw that orange juice was seeping through my fingers dripping down onto my coat. I opened my hand to examine the orange, but all that remained was a messy pulp. Before I could clean up the mess, I heard more rustling through the bushes. I looked up just in time to see three more boys were standing there, along with a girl, all five now watching me intently. I started to feel nervous, but before I could do or say anything, the tallest boy with spiky red hair and freckles nodded at me, then turned to face the rest.

"Let's go." With that they all started heading towards the school with not a single backward glance, not that I expected them to. I just wanted to take one more look into the blue-green eyes of the first boy; they were so mesmerising.

After school, I sat on a wall near the school gates waiting for Kasey-Ray. I was not surprised to see her walking out surrounded by admirers.

"Erin!" She shouted loudly, making everyone look from her to me. I wanted the ground to open up and swallow me where I sat. We walked to the gates and came to a halt; I shuffled impatiently from one foot to the other as I waited for her to say her goodbyes.

I glanced around. The boy I had seen earlier, getting into the passenger seat of a black Fiat Punto with two of the boys and the girl that I'd seen with him. The boy with the spiky red hair was leaning against the car talking to him whilst looking around, obviously searching for someone. Then his eyes met mine and I quickly looked away, embarrassed that I'd been caught staring.

Kasey-Ray still hadn't finished her goodbyes, and from the corner of my eye, I spotted the red haired girl, from my form room.

She hadn't spotted me, but I watched her curiously, as she walked towards the car park and straight to them.

That was who the tall spiky-haired boy had been looking for. He put his arm around her and kissed the top of her head, and for once she looked like she was smiling.

I slowly looked back to the boy in the passenger seat and he was looking right at me. My heart sped up. He quickly looked away and I felt her eyes burning into me furiously.

Jessica Watson. I'd learnt that much from form room today. I noticed the spiky-haired boy pulling her away as the boy in the passenger seat stared down at the road, like he was day dreaming.

"Ready?" The sound of Kasey-Ray's voice made me jump. I quickly looked at her.

She was looking at the car with the good looking boy in it as it pulled away.

"Who was that?" She looked me with a smile.

"No idea," I shrugged, as she looked at me thoughtfully, then smiled.

"Okay, let's go."

***

The next day, I walked into my form room and sat straight at my table at the back of the room, ignoring the stares from my fellow classmates

"Who the hell do you think you are?" boomed Jessica, as she stormed to where I sat. I opened my mouth to try and speak. Before I could find the words, she shoved my table into me, nearly sending me backwards in my chair. Luckily there was a wall behind me to stop me falling.

"Listen you freak!"

I swallowed hard, trying not to cry. My ribs were hurting from the impact with the table, and I was turning beetroot from everyone staring and laughing.

"I want you to stay away from Sean. Don't look at him or think about him, and if you see him, you best walk the other way!"

Sean? That was his name?   The sound of his name gave me goose bumps.

"Hey, I'm talking to you." Jessica pushed the table again. Not as hard this time, but hard enough that I had to bite my lip, to stop from crying out. "Do I make myself clear?" She leaned forwards and glared at me, all I could do was nod.

Then she turned to walk back to her own table, just as Ms Forrester walked through the door.

***

At lunchtime it was raining outside, so I went and sat at a table in the far corner by myself, ignoring everyone looking at me. I knew eventually they would get bored and find some other monster to stare at. Well, I hoped so anyway.

I had just finished my lunch, and was thinking about how I would get through my lessons this afternoon. Science followed by P.E. Not my favourite subjects, to say the least.

"No oranges today?" I jumped and looked up to see Sean standing at my table.

"N-n-no." I managed to stutter, as my cheeks flushed bright red. I looked past him to see most people staring and whispering.

"I suppose that's a good thing." He waited until I looked back at him, "We don't want any more oranges being murdered now, do we?" He tilted his head to the side and smiled. It was the first time I'd seen him smile. It made his eyes sparkle. He was even more beautiful when he smiled.

I nervously glanced down at the table. When my eyes returned to his, the smile had gone, but his eyes were still warm and inviting.

He continued to look at me, like there was something he wanted to ask.

"Jacko?" Someone shouted from the other end of the lunch room, making him look behind him. He was about to walk away, but slowly turned back to me.

"Nice seeing you again!" Then he turned and walked away.

I was still staring after him, when I noticed Kasey-Ray trying to catch my eye. She smiled, waved, and then pointed to her watch. I looked down at mine and saw I had just five minutes to get to class.

***

I managed to get through Science easy enough. It took a lot to try and listen to what the teacher was saying. My mind kept going back to Sean.

His beautiful face, eyes you could swim in, and a smile that could break hearts.

Before I knew it, class was over and it was time for P.E. I wasn't the sportiest of people and would rather sit on the sidelines and watch.

Walking into the changing rooms, I placed my coat and bag on a peg. I was about to start getting changed when my head slammed against one of the pegs and I fell to the floor. I looked up to see Jessica standing over me.

"What did I tell you?"

Tears welled up in my eyes, nausea was creeping up on me, my head was throbbing and I tasted blood in my mouth, from where I was biting my lip to stop myself from crying.

Before I could reply, Mrs Taylor appeared wondering what was keeping us all. She saw me slumped on the floor, blood dripping down the side of my head.

"What happened?" She asked, as she pushed through the other students, who were crowding around me.

By this time, the blood was on my white school shirt and Mrs Taylor was looking around at the other girls faces, demanding to know what had happened.

"She fell and hit her head on the pegs." I heard Jessica purr innocently. Mrs Taylor looked back to me.

"Is Jessica telling the truth?" Even though she asked this, her voice was full of scepticism. I nodded and started to pull myself up.

"Exactly what she said."

Jessica gave a smug smile, and then turned back to Mrs Taylor.

"I can take her to the nurse's office, if you like?" She smiled like butter wouldn't melt in her mouth.

Mrs Taylor sighed, and after looking back and forth between us, she finally spoke.

"Okay. Jessica, you take her there and come straight back."

For a while Jessica and I walked in silence. Her hands gripped tightly to the top of my right arm, her nails digging through my shirt.

Just before we got to the nurse's office, she spun me around and threw me against the wall, placing one hand on my throat, and the other she traced down the front of my body, stopping once or twice to jab her finger into me.

"I won't tell you again." She spat, her face so close to mine I could feel her warm breath. "Next time, it won't be the nurse's office you end up in!"

I felt warm liquid trickle down my legs. Jessica must have smelt it, as she quickly released me after giving me a final shove against the wall. She looked from the puddle on the floor, then back to me.

"You disgust me." She said with pure venom. I couldn't understand the hatred she felt towards me. But I did know that I would stay as far away from Sean as I possibly could.

Luckily the cut on my head wasn't as bad as it looked. Kasey-Ray was called out of her class to walk me home. Which she was extremely grateful for, because she hated geography and as her teacher spoke in a monotonous tone, she was close to falling asleep when the nurse came to rescue her.

I told Kasey-Ray the same story Jessica had told Mrs Taylor. I had fallen; she seemed to believe me and didn't question me further.

I still couldn't understand why Jessica hated me so much. From the second I had entered my form room, she had glared at me with pure hatred in her eyes and this was before I'd even laid eyes on Sean. Why did she want me to stay away from him? Why would she feel threatened by someone like me? It wasn't as if he would ever find me attractive. I was a freak and the huge birthmark on the side of my face showed this. He could have anyone he wanted. I didn't know why he even took the time of day to talk to me.

Another thing, he looked too old to even be at school. Whenever I saw him and his friends, they never had school uniform on. So why would they be on the school grounds, let alone be inside the school?

Why on the first day I met him, did he and his friends come through the bushes?

My emotions were all over the place. At first, I was scared and hurt, and then I was confused, now I was starting to feel annoyed. It's not like I had asked for this attention. Most people ran a mile when they saw me.

He didn't even seem to notice the ugly birthmark on my face. Or, if he had noticed it, he had never looked at it. Whenever he looked at me, he looked deep into my eyes. It was as if he was searching for the answer to some unspoken question.

We had only just turned into our street when my Mum came flying out of the front door.

"Erin!" She cried, running towards us. "I'm sorry, your Dad and I were out shopping when the school rang, or we would have come to collect you." She told me as she started to examine me, right there in the street.

"Mum, I'm fine!" I tried to reassure her, as Kasey-Ray continued walking to the house. "I fell, it looks worse than it is."

"You need to be more careful!" She exclaimed, horrified at the sight of the blood in my hair. She ushered me into the house, where my Dad was waiting. He looked like he had been pacing the floors.

"Erin!" He rushed towards me, trying to hug me.

"Dad, I'm fine!" I sighed, holding my hands up. I felt like a stuck record having to repeat myself over and over again. I just hoped they bought the whole falling excuse.

My Dad looked to my Mum. I didn't see the look she gave him, but he sighed and stepped back. "I just fell Dad, there was a bag on the floor and I didn't see it." He nodded and looked like he believed every word I said. "Do you think it's ok if I have a wash?" I turned to ask my Mum.

She hesitated for a moment.

"As long as you don't get anything in the cut. Tell you what. I'll help you wash your hair." She offered, and then followed me as I nodded.

I took my coat off and carried my rucksack to my room. After taking off my shirt and throwing it into the washing basket, I slipped on an old t-shirt, and then headed to the bathroom, where my Mum was waiting.

Without a word I leant over the bath, my Mum gently poured warm water over my head. I watched as pools of red swirled around and finally escaped down the plug hole.

"I'm not going to shampoo your hair. Not today. I want to wait until that heals a bit more." She said as she placed a towel on my head gently.

"Okay." I told her, as I watched the final drops of blood disappear. "I'm just going to clean my face, then do my homework."

My Mum hesitated in the doorway for a while. It seemed something was on her mind. The telephone rang then, making her shake her head.

"Okay love, I'll call you when dinner is ready."

I walked into my bedroom, leaning against the door as I closed it. I closed my eyes and just stood there, tears started to roll down my face as I slid down the door to the floor and I sat there for at least 30 minutes, just crying.

I can't believe she did that. I thought as I placed my head in my hands.

For years I'd grown up hardly talking to anyone besides my family, and now that someone, who I was interested in getting to know, had started talking to me, I was supposed to steer clear of him.

I felt my stomach tighten at this thought. But I had to; I couldn't have any more run-ins with Jessica. I didn't know Sean well enough to put my life in danger.

God I'm so stupid! Why was I even thinking through this? I had to stay away from Sean. End of.

I wiped away my tears, and with a deep breath stood up and walked over to my rucksack, I pulled out my reading material. I must have fallen asleep, as I woke when someone started to gently shake me. I yawned and stretched, then opened my eyes.

"*Kes*?" My Dad was sitting flicking through the book I'd brought home from school. "Interesting read." He smiled as he placed it back down.

"It's for English," I smiled back. "I've got to read it by next Tuesday." I pulled myself up into a sitting position and placed the book on my bedside table.

"I nearly forgot what I came in here for," My Dad said, shaking his head with a laugh, "Dinner's ready."

"Okay, I'll be down in a second. I just need to use the toilet."

My Dad nodded as he got up from the bed and headed downstairs.

After a quick trip to the bathroom, I made my way to the kitchen, where I heard Kasey-Ray talking excitedly about the new friends she'd made.

She'd gotten close to a girl called Claire, who was in her form and most of her classes.

"So can she come here after school tomorrow?" She gave my parents her big puppy dog eyes impression.

My parents laughed as they nodded. "Yay!" She clapped and looked over at me as I walked in. "Hi sis, how's your head?"

"It's good thanks." I smiled as I sat opposite her at the kitchen table.

My Mum had made Spaghetti Bolognese, my favourite and sitting in the middle of the table was a plate of garlic bread.

"So what's Claire like?" I enjoyed finding out all about Kasey-Ray's friends. It was the closest I'd get to having friends myself, not that Kasey-Ray's friends really spoke to me, just a polite hello now and again.

"Oh she's great." Kasey-Ray beamed, "You'll love her."

"I'm sure I will." Laughing, knowing full well I wouldn't. Most were nice to my face, but steered clear of me anytime Kasey-Ray wasn't around.

I all but licked my plate clean as I finished my dinner.

"Thanks," I smiled as I pushed my plate away and rubbed my belly. "That was lush." I stood up and took my plate over to the sink. "I'm going to go read some more."

My parents nodded and turned back to listen to Kasey-Ray chatter on about school. I slowly made my way to my bedroom; I was trying to decide whether to put my pyjamas on now or not. I finally decided to put them on. That way, if I did fall asleep, I would already be dressed for bed.

I pulled my favourite pyjamas on, which I'd had for three years now. I had grown out of them 2 years ago, but I just loved them. Every morning I would take them off, fold them and then place them under my pillow, to keep them warm.

After brushing my teeth, I climbed into bed and picked up my book but it wasn't long before I fell asleep.

Chapter 3

That night, I dreamt of my first day at school, when I'd sat eating my lunch on the school field.

Sean had just appeared in front of me.

"I wouldn't let her get to you!" He told me this time, making me jump. He hadn't said that the first time I'd met him.

When he looked down at my hand, I already knew that I would see the messy pulp of the orange. But when I looked down at my hand I saw blood. I looked back at Sean in alarm as four people appeared behind him, but these weren't the same people I'd seen in the field. Their heads were all Jessica's. I tried to move away from her enraged face. Her red hair furiously licked like flames around her.

"I warned you!" She screamed. I looked back at Sean for help, but he was Sean no more, he was Jessica.

Seeing the confusion in my face, all the Jessica's started laughing. Scrambling to my feet and leaving everything behind, I ran. All the time their laughter was ringing in my ears.

As I got near the school, the other students were laughing and pointing. My heart was beating fast. I still had blood on my hand, but from where? I saw the back of Kasey-Ray, as she stood talking to her friends. I reached out to touch her and she spun around, making me fall to the floor. This wasn't my sister, it was Jessica, and she was leaning over me, trying to claw at me.

I lay there on the floor, curled up in a ball and screamed.

"Erin?" A voice broke my scream as they shook me "Erin?" They called again.

Slowly I opened my eyes and cried out with relief when I saw my Mum sitting on my bed.

"Oh Mum." I sobbed.

"Hey, it's okay, you're safe now." She soothed. "But we need to sort your head out."

I quickly jumped up to see blood on my bed. I looked down at the hand I'd held the orange in and saw that was covered in blood too.

"Oh my god, what happened?" I screamed hysterically.

"I think you were having a nightmare and you must have scratched your cut!" She stood up and put her arm around me, as she placed a towel to my head. "Your Dad is just getting dressed; he's going to take you to the hospital. You're going to need stitches!"

I nodded, still crying. My dream had felt so real.

My Mum guided me down the stairs where my Dad was waiting. She helped me put my coat and trainers on as I sat there in a daze. My mind was flashing back and forth between my nightmare and reality. My Mum kissed my cheek and gave me a hug. She looked so worried and tired.

"Come on sweetie, get you in the car." My Dad soothed. "I'll text when we're leaving." He leant over and gave my Mum a kiss. She nodded as she kissed her fingers and placed them to my cheek. I thought she was going to cry.

For most of the journey, my Dad and I sat in silence. I sat there with the towel pressed tightly to my head, scared that if I moved it, blood would come pouring out.

"What were you dreaming about?" He finally asked, breaking the silence. He was trying to pretend that he wasn't too bothered what it was about.

"Rats!" I'd been sitting in silence for so long that I was able to come up with the perfect nightmare.

"Rats, eh?" My Dad nodded, not taking his eyes off the road. I wasn't sure if he believed me or not, so I thought I would elaborate, as I knew my Dad feared them as much as I did.

"Yeah, there were lots of them, and they were crawling all over me and trying to eat me." I saw my Dad shiver and instantly I knew he believed me.

"I think I would have screamed too!" He gave me a nervous laugh. He looked relieved when he saw the turning for the hospital car park.

We didn't have to wait too long to be seen. Unfortunately I did need stitches, which meant that they had to shave off some hair around the cut. Luckily, I had the rest of my hair to cover it.

"Three stitches!" My Dad said. He had decided to phone my Mum, instead of texting. "Yeah, she's fine, just tired. I think she will be asleep before we get home." He laughed. "Ok baby, I'll see you soon. I love you!" Then he blew a kiss and hung up the phone. "Ready?" He turned to look at me and I nodded. I was really tired, but I wasn't going to fall asleep, mainly because I felt I needed to keep my Dad awake so we got home safely. Also, I was too scared to fall asleep, in case I dreamt of her again.

"You ever read *Kes* before Dad?" he shook his head as he fastened his seat belt.

"No, but I did see the film years ago."

"Really? Mr Clarke wants us to finish our book by Tuesday, so we can watch the movie." My Dad laughed. "What's funny?"

"When I was a kid, our English teacher said the same thing."

"And?" I didn't see why that was funny.

"Well, most of us thought, why bother with the book if we are going the see the movie!" he winked.

"Ah, I see!" I could see his point.

"But, on the downside, he gave us a test on the book!" He laughed again.

"How did you do? Or needn't I ask?" I laughed too.

"Let's say, I didn't get a C or above." We both laughed as he turned into our street and pulled into the driveway.

"Damn!" I said as I went to get out of the car

"What's wrong sweetie?"

"I left the towel at the hospital." Dad was laughing again.

"I think you did your Mum a favour," he winked.

It was dark inside the house, apart from the landing light. We slowly and quietly climbed the stairs, hoping not to wake anyone, but my Mum was already awake, we saw her coming out of my bedroom.

"Hi love!" She smiled. She looked relieved to see me smiling. "How are you feeling?"

"Tired!" I yawned.

"Well, I've changed your bed covers and switched your alarm off. No school for you tomorrow." I wanted to tap dance when I heard the last bit. "Sleep as long as you want, and I'll try to keep Kasey-Ray quiet."

Walking into my bedroom, I expected to see a scene from a horror movie, but my room was back to normal, no blood anywhere.

I climbed into bed and looked at my clock, 3:57am. *Ouch!* I thought. No *wonder Mum said no school tomorrow*.

I was too tired to fight sleep. When I did fall asleep, I didn't dream. Well I couldn't remember dreaming. I just knew that I felt rested as I slowly opened my eyes and looked at my clock, 11:33am. *Wow, I slept half the day away*. I lay there for another 30 minutes, not wanting to leave my warm cosy bed, but my bladder felt like it had its own alarm and was screaming at me to go to the bathroom.

No sooner had I finished than my stomach gave a loud rumble. *Give me a break*, I thought. I just wanted to go back to bed. It rumbled again in reply, making me laugh as I opened the bathroom door and saw my Dad coming out of his bedroom, full dressed in his work clothes.

"What's funny?" He smiled at me.

"My belly is talking to me." We both laughed as it rumbled again in reply, 1 then I raised my eyebrow. "You off to work?"

"Yeah, Mr Thomas's boiler has broken and Alan is out on another job."

Alan Urban was my Dad's boss. He owned Galladale's only plumbing business and he was a one man band until my Dad came along, he had hired my Dad on the spot.

"Okay Dad, I'm just going to go get something to eat."

"Okay sweetie, I'll see you later!" With that he gave me a quick kiss and rushed out of the house, grabbing his tools that were next to the front door, whilst I headed to the kitchen to raid the cupboards.

I finally settled on a bowl of cereal and sat at the table mindlessly flipping through today's paper whilst eating. After I finished, I took my bowl to the sink and proceeded to look through the junk food cupboard, pulling out a large bag of bacon fries and a bar of chocolate, then turned to the fridge to pull out a bottle of Dr Pepper.

"These will do nicely," I said out loud, as I headed back to my room to watch a DVD.

After thumbing through my DVD collection, I decided to watch 'The Goonies.' had ended up becoming my favourite movie after I had sat and watched it with my Mum when I was younger.

It was nearing the end when I heard Kasey-Ray come home from school. Two sets of feet climbed the stairs as I remembered that she was bringing her friend Claire over.

"My room's through there. I won't be long. I just wanna speak to Erin." Then I heard a knock on my door. "Can I come in?" She asked as she closed the door behind her and came to sit on my bed, stealing a bacon fry in the process.

"Hey!"

"What?" She replied, trying to look innocent which made me laugh.

"What's up?" I paused my DVD player and turned to look at her. Obviously she had something on her mind.

"I heard something today!"

"Uh-huh," not really understanding what this had to do with me.

"Did you really fall or did that bitch, Jessica, push you?" She just came out with it, causing me to almost choke on a bacon fry.

"Don't tell Mum and Dad, please?" I begged.

"I won't, but I have a good mind to kick her head in." She was really angry, probably with me too for lying to her. "Why didn't you tell me?" I shrugged, wanting to cry.

For most of the day I'd blocked out what had happened.

"Don't go crying on me," She stroked the top of the covers where my legs were. "I heard it was because she wants you to stay away from some lad." All I could do was nod. "Look, don't let her get to you, I've got your back!" She moved closer and gave me a hug. "I promise I won't tell Mum and Dad, just promise me you'll tell me if she does anything again, okay?" I nodded as she stood up. I was supposed to be the big sister looking out for her, not the other way round. "Love you!" She called as she shut the door.

"Love you more!" I shouted after her.

***

The next day I went back to school, scared sick was an understatement. I thought I was going to have a panic attack when we got near the school gates.

The usual people had stopped to stare; some even laughing and pointing. I flinched when I heard them mention Jessica's name.

"You got nothing better to do?" Kasey-Ray snapped, making everyone turn away.

Lowering my head, I let Kasey-Ray steer me through the school gates and to the main doors. "I'll meet you here right after school, okay?"

"Okay," I nodded as I began the long walk to my form room.

Taking a deep breath, I walked into the room and went straight to my desk, deliberately avoiding eye contact with anyone and everyone.

Only 30 minutes, I thought. I wished all my lessons were this short, but form room was just a formality, so the teacher could take the register, let us know of any upcoming events and changes to our time-tables.

I sat at my table, with my rucksack in-between my body and table, pretending to look for something. I just wanted to have something there, in case she decided she hadn't finished with me yet and another shove of the table was in order. Also I wanted to look preoccupied, so I couldn't catch anyone's attention, especially Jessica's. I heard her enter the room and people surrounded her, those who wouldn't normally give her the time of day. Maybe they were scared of her, or just wanted to pat her on the back for hitting the school freak, either way I was just happy that the attention had shifted away from me. Even if it was probably, only momentarily.

After Ms Forrester had called out our names, she closed the register and started writing on the black board.

SCHOOL SPORT'S DAY

Most of the class groaned, apart from a couple who lived for sport's day and all other types of sporting events.

"I am going to need two people to represent our form in every event, with the exception of the relay, which I will need four." She paced left and right, across the front of the classroom making eye contact with every student. "I would like it if everyone could participate, but for those who don't, you will be expected to help out on the various stalls. Is that clear?" She stopped to look long and hard at us.

"Yes Miss!" We all chorused.

"I will write a list of events on the board and I want those of you who are interested to raise their hands, and on Monday we will get it down to the right amount." She turned back to the black board as she starting to write down all the events. I knew there was no way I was raising my hand up to any of them.

Jessica's hand, however, was raised for every running race, including the hurdles. I had heard the others saying that no one stood a chance against Jessica; she was the fastest in the whole school and had won every race, every year.

"Well, that's it!" Ms Forrester concluded. "I will see you all Monday morning and we can put it to a vote." She headed to her desk as everyone started packing up to leave. I took my time, as I didn't want to hang around outside my classroom. I would rather take the allocated time between classes and get there just as the teacher was arriving to let us in.

"Erin?" Ms Forrester called as I was just about to leave, "Do you have a minute?"

"Yes Miss!" She could have as many minutes as she liked.

"I just wanted to see how you are. How's your head?"

"It's fine. I caught it in my sleep on Wednesday night and had to have stitches, but it's fine now."

"Yes, I received the letter from your mother yesterday." She looked at me thoughtfully. "Are you settling in okay? Making friends?"

"Yes Miss!" She looked at me again like she was judging my reaction, but I wasn't going to tell her that I hated school, I hated the other students and most of the time I hated the fact I'd been born.

"Well, if there's ever anything you want to discuss. I want you to know that I am always here to listen." She smiled sweetly, covering her defeated expression.

"Yes Miss, Thank you."

"Okay, you best get to your class."

This morning I had Science, followed by French, then after lunch Maths followed by Art.

I really enjoyed Art. I loved how there was no right or wrong, I could express myself however I chose fit, without anyone criticising me.

Before I knew it, it was home time. I picked up my bag and headed towards the main doors to meet Kasey-Ray. I was glad the day was over, and more relieved that Jessica hadn't said or done anything. She had acted like I didn't exist and this suited me fine.

Walking through the doors, I spotted Kasey-Ray standing with her friend Claire; they were talking to a group of boys. She saw me as soon as I walked through the doors. "Gotta go," She quickly told them. "See ya Monday!" She called, "Claire, I'll call you tonight!" She gave Claire a quick wink as she linked arms with me. "He is so hot!" She drooled as she squeezed my arm.

"Who?"

"The tall one." I looked past her towards the boy's she was just with, "Don't look!"

"Nice." I told her. He was no Sean, but he wasn't bad looking.

"Was he looking?" I laughed at my sister as she blushed. So much for her not wanting me to look.

"Yeah, he was!" She smiled a huge triumphant smile.

"He is just so gorgeous."

We walked in silence, arm in arm, as I left her to her own thoughts. As we walked past the school car park, I kept my eyes looking straight ahead. I didn't want to catch a glimpse of Sean; I knew I could not deal with the consequences. I would just have to squash this little crush I had on him.

One guy shows a little bit of interest and I go all gooey, I sighed and shook my head.

"You okay?" Kasey-Ray asked as we walked through the school gates.

"Yeah fine," I smiled. "Why wouldn't I be?"

"Hmmm..." She didn't look convinced.

"What?"

"She didn't say anything to you today, did she?"

"Nope, she didn't even look at me!" and that was the truth. I just hoped it would continue like this.

The problem with having no friends was that it gave me a lot of time to think, or rather daydream. I would often find myself thinking about Sean. I even, absent-mindedly, caught myself doodling his name and straight away I would screw up the piece of paper and throw it in the bin.

I had even thought about joining one of those social network sites that Kasey-Ray was on, just to see if I could find him and see if he had any pictures, if he had a girlfriend, and anything else I could find out, but what was the point? Didn't you need to have friends for those websites? Who would I have as my friends? Kasey-Ray? My Mum? Or maybe even my Dad?

"Pathetic!" I said out loud, screwing another doodle up and throwing it in the bin.

"What's pathetic?" Kasey-Ray asked as she breezed through the door.

"Oh nothing, I was just trying to draw something for Art but it wasn't good enough," I quickly said.

"Let me have a look," she walked towards the bin, but I quickly jumped up and blocked her.

"No, no it's okay. What was it you wanted?"

"Oh right, yes." She was easily distracted. "Mum and Dad are just going to grab some DVD's and pizza and asked if we wanted to go. I said yes, mainly because they will probably choose something totally lame."

"Okay," I laughed as I switched off my lamp and followed her down the stairs.

Every Friday night my family and I always tried to have a movie night. Sometimes my Dad was called to work or Kasey-Ray had made plans, so it would end up being my Mum and me, and my Mum would watch anything I wanted to, which was great.

Grabbing my coat from the cupboard, I quickly jumped into the back seat of my parent's car, next to Kasey-Ray.

"Did your form teacher mention sport's day today?" Kasey-Ray asked as she fastened her seatbelt.

"Yep, but I'm not taking part."

"Why not?" She scoffed without waiting for an answer, "I put my name down for everything." She laughed, sounding really excited.

"I'll just help selling drinks or something. That's the best my athletic ability will stretch?" I laughed as she rolled her eyes.

It didn't take long before we arrived at the DVD shop. Kasey-Ray and I quickly jumped out and ran to the new releases as our parents headed off to a different section. Kasey-Ray was quick to decide what she wanted and went off to find our parents to show them what she had chosen, whilst I carried on looking. I must have looked for a good few minutes but there was nothing that I fancied. I'd seen most of them. I turned around, ready to go find my family but I wasn't looking where I was going and bumped into someone as I walked past.

"Oh sorry." I Mumbled, not looking up as I quickly tried to hurry past.

"No worries." It was the sound of his voice that stopped me, making me turn back, as my heart jumped to my mouth.

It was Sean, and from what I could tell, he was alone. I don't think he realised it was me, or probably didn't even care. He didn't look back, as he walked out and climbed into the driver's seat of a bright orange Ford Focus ST. As soon as he was in he seemed to sense someone was watching him and he looked straight at me, making me panic and quickly turn away, knocking into my Dad, making him drop the DVD's in his hands.

"Sorry Dad!" I took a deep breath trying to slow my heart rate down. He didn't seem to notice the panic in my face. ?Are we going now?"

"Yes why? You okay?" He raised an eyebrow and put a hand on my forehead like he was checking my temperature.

"Yeah fine, just really hungry." Forcing a smile. He laughed as he put his arm around me.

"Just going to pay for these, then we'll go get a pizza."

"Mmmm yum." Forcing enthusiasm into my voice. I actually felt sick. I hoped Jessica and the others weren't with him. Oh god, I thought, starting to feel panicked.

"Your Mum and sister are just grabbing some popcorn, you can grab something to eat now if you're that hungry." My Dad suggested.

"No it's ok, I'll wait."

***

By the time we'd gotten home, I'd calmed down. I'd reasoned with myself that he probably didn't realise it was me.

I managed to force down four slices of ham, mushroom and pepperoni pizza as I sat curled up on the sofa.

By the time the second movie had finished I was tired and there was no way I could make it through the third.

"I'm off to bed!" I yawned as I stretched.

"But we have another one to watch!" Kasey-Ray looked wide awake. She could probably watch another two or three movies before she started to feel sleepy.

"I'll watch it tomorrow, or you can tell me all about it." I laughed as I ruffled her hair. "Night." I leaned over to give each of them a kiss. "I love you all!"

"Love you too!" They chorused.

Once I climbed into bed, I fell straight asleep and it was not long before I was dreaming about him.

We were back in the DVD shop again, but this time when I knocked into him, he lifted his arms and placed them on me, stopping me from moving, then he leaned down to kiss me. His lips were mere centimetres away from mine when I heard a loud banging coming from the shop window.

"I warned you!" I heard Jessica hiss, making me jump away from Sean. She was furious as she pounded on the glass. Everything around me slowly disappeared leaving me standing in a darkened room. Jessica was still pounding on the window. The banging noise was pulling me from the darkened room and dream. My eyes opened and the familiar surroundings of my bedroom came into view. Then I heard the banging again. It was coming from my window. I couldn't see who it was as my curtains were shut and I was too scared to go and look, because I knew it would be Jessica. She had found out that I'd seen Sean and come to deliver her warning.

Pulling my knees up to my chest, I rocked myself back and forth. I was so scared. I wanted to scream but there was no sound.

Then my bedroom door swung open, making me catch my voice and scream as the light switched on.

It was my Dad and he stood there half asleep wearing just his boxer shorts and a t-shirt.

"What's going on?" He demanded, rubbing his eyes as he looked from me to the window, but all I could do was shake my head and start crying.

My Mum wasn't far behind him and she quickly came to sit beside me, placing an arm around my back.

Taking a deep breath, whilst shaking with nerves, my Dad stepped towards my window and pulled my curtains open. Then he sighed and started to laugh nervously.

"Stupid tree!"

He slowly opened my window, carefully trying not to let the wind pull it from his hands, as he reached out and snapped a few branches off the tree and threw them to the ground outside.

"There!" He closed the window and shut my curtains, looking relieved. "I'll take off a few more branches tomorrow. You try and get some sleep." He walked over and gave me a kiss, then left with my Mum to go back to bed.

No matter how hard I tried, I just couldn't get back to sleep. Rather than switching on my TV, I decided to go downstairs and watch TV there, and that's where my Mum found me at 7:30am, fast asleep on the sofa.

"Morning," She cheerily said as she sat down to change the channel, after placing a blanket on me. "How long have you been down here for?"

"Dunno," I shrugged with a yawn.

"Your Dad and I are going for a walk later, if you want to come?"

"Maybe." I was that tired, I didn't have the energy to talk. The next thing I knew it was after 10am and Kasey-Ray was sat next to me.

"You don't half snore." She teased. She ducked out of the way, as I launched a pillow at her. I lazily got up off the sofa and padded up to the bathroom. After brushing my teeth and washing my face, I went to my room and straight to my window, to see where the noises were coming from. I didn't feel scared, maybe because it was daylight, but I needn't have worried; it was my Dad. He was up the ladder, sawing at the tree. He caught a glimpse of me waving and smiled; I turned back to find some clothes.

Chapter 4

The weekend went by pretty quickly. On Saturday, I went for a walk with my parents and on Sunday, I spent most of my time in my room, finishing off my book for English.

On Monday morning we got to school fifteen minutes earlier than normal, so Kasey-Ray and I sat on the wall next to the car park waiting for Claire. I could have just gone to my form room when we got to school, but I decided I would rather be with my sister and get to my form room at the last minute, just in case Jessica knew I'd bumped into Sean. If I got there just as Ms Forrester did, then I would buy myself more time. But she didn't bother me at all.

In form room it was decided that I would sell programmes with Ms Forrester on sport's day, which suited me just fine. Jessica was going to take part in every event she wanted, which seemed to make her happy.

Sport's day was only a month away; it was the day before school finished for the summer holidays. Everyone knew that it would soon fly by. I was looking forward to not having to come to school, as I always felt like I was walking on eggshells. It wouldn't be so bad if I ran into Sean, as I wouldn't have to face Jessica in school the next day. Not that I would run into him, I was just secretly hoping I would. It was harder to catch glimpses of him when I saw him on the school grounds. I was sure someone would report back to Jessica, just because they loved the thrill of seeing someone being hurt by another.

After that day in the girl's changing room, it was like I didn't exist. No one spoke to me, and most people stopped looking at me.

Even after school, when I saw Sean and his friends in the car park, waiting for Jessica, it was rare any of them would look in my direction.

By now I'd learnt all of their names. Justin Michaels was the tall, spiky, red haired boy. He was Jessica's 18 year old boyfriend.

Apparently, none of them attended Galladale High School; they went to the community college next to the school. This would probably explain why I'd seen them come through the bushes.

The other two boys were Paul and James Hunter. Identical twins who had just turned 18. I couldn't tell them apart, and apparently no one else could either, apart from Kelly Jackson. She was the girl who was always with them. She was a plain looking girl, but pretty at the same time. She had long brown hair with a stripe of purple on one side, and a stripe of blue on the other. I'd overheard someone saying she was going out with one of the twins, but no-one knew which. The most interesting thing I found out about her was that she is the older sister of Sean.

Sean was the youngest in the group, apart from Jessica.

The rumours were that when he was at high school, he was very popular. Captain of most sport's teams and always had a different girl each week. Then in his last year of high school, he had returned to school, after the Easter holiday and had changed.

He wasn't really interested in sport's any more, and he wouldn't look at any of the girls, let alone talk to them. He would just sit still with the same group of friends he had grown up with. Instead of being the main one involved in the conversations, he would just sit there in silence.

It was his friends outside of school that intrigued everyone, Justin, Paul and James. They'd been in the year above Sean, with his sister, and he'd never once spoken to any of them.

You see, Justin, Paul and James weren't exactly popular, like Sean and Kelly. So no-one could figure out why they had become friends.

It was only after a few weeks, when people started noticing Kelly with Paul and James, waiting for Sean.

No one was entirely sure how Jessica fitted into their little group. I had overheard people referring to her as their guard dog. Not that they would ever say that to her face.

The week seemed to fly by. There was a buzz in the air, about the upcoming sport's day, with the general banter of who would beat who.

The form room in every year, which had the most points, would win a trophy and their form name would be put up in reception. Every year, my form room had won it for our year, so I was glad I wasn't taking part. I didn't want to be the one responsible for letting the whole class down.

By Friday I was feeling happy. The buzz from the other students must have rubbed off on me. Plus, I hadn't had any problems with Jessica.

As Kasey-Ray and I walked home from school, I listened intently as Kasey-Ray told me that her form room had never won the trophy.

Best they'd ever done is second. But I reckon we can win it this year, because I've run against Sophie in P.E and I beat her every time"

Sophie Roberts was in a different form room from Kasey-Ray, and even though they sat at the same table for lunch and break, there seemed to be a bit of a rivalry forming.

"I don't think she is used to being beaten." Kasey-Ray laughed, "I wonder how she'll feel about losing in front of the whole school."

"She'll probably throw her teddies out of the cot, by the sound of it!" I laughed.

We were two streets from our house when I spotted an orange car slowly drive past, going in the opposite direction, making my heart start to speed up. I would recognise that car anywhere.

Every time I saw his car, or caught a glimpse of him, it would set my pulse racing, and now it was going like the clappers, as it turned around and drove past again. I had no idea where he lived, so I didn't know if he was heading home or not. *Why did he go one way, then turn and go in the direction we were headed?*

Just before we turned into our street, I noticed he'd pulled to the side of the road, the engine still running. If I had more courage, I would have walked over to see if he needed help or something.

As soon as we turned into our street, I heard the sound of his tyres squealing as he sped away.

Kasey-Ray had been oblivious to it all. She was still going on about sport's day. I smiled to myself. I should have felt frightened when I saw Sean's car, but it was only his car I'd seen. Jessica hadn't said anything about me not looking at his car.

She may, however, have mentioned that I couldn't think about him, but I never stopped thinking about him and she'd never pulled me up on it. It wasn't like she was a mind reader. If she was, she wasn't very good at it.

I was still daydreaming about him when we got home. I sighed as my Dad broke into my thoughts.

"Do you have home-work girls?" He asked as soon as we stepped through the door.

"I do." I told him as I went to put my coat away.

"Not me." Kasey-Ray cheerily added. She probably did, but would only remember last minute, on Sunday night.

"We'll go grab some DVD's as soon as you're finished." He informed me as he carried a pile of washing upstairs.

I only had maths to do and I was finished in an hour.

"Done!" I called as I ran down the stairs, almost tripping over Kasey-Ray's shoes that she had abandoned at the bottom.

On the way there, I was lost in my own thoughts, wondering if I'd see him there again. As we pulled into an empty parking space, I quickly scanned the area, hoping to see his car. Unfortunately, I didn't. Sighing I followed my family inside and went straight to the new releases with Kasey-Ray. It didn't take long for Kasey-Ray to find something she wanted to watch, as she picked up a film called 'Four Lions'.

"This is supposed to be hilarious." She exclaimed, as she flipped it over to look at the back. "You decided yet?"

"No, still looking." I said, shaking my head.

"Okay, I'll go see what the olds are getting." I nodded as I continued to look through the hundreds of new releases, then one jumped out at me. Maybe it was because I found the actor, Jake Gyllenhaal, to be quite good looking, but I liked the sound of the title. 'Love and other drugs.' Picking it up, I flipped it over and started reading the back.

"Supposed to be good." The sound of his voice made me freeze. "My sister watched it the other day." I didn't know what to say. I managed to look up at him with a shy smile as I blushed. "Sorry, I didn't mean to intrude." He looked away, looking slightly embarrassed.

"Did you sister like it then?" I managed a dry squeak. He looked pleased that I'd responded, as he turned back towards me.

"Yeah!" He smiled. "Something about having some gorgeous actor in it." I blushed again, knowing this was one of the reasons I was getting it. I was now in two minds, whether or not to get it. "Are you getting it then?" He seemed to sense my indecisiveness.

"I don't know." I was until he spoke.

"You should, and then you can tell me if it's any good." His smile was genuine. I liked the sound of that, but I had to think about Jessica.

Just then his phone went; he pulled it out of his back pocket to read his message.

"I've got to go." He put his phone away. "I expect a full report next Friday!" Then he left. I was still standing there, staring after him, as Kasey-Ray came back over.

"Are you getting that then?" I turned to smile at her as I nodded.

"I think I am."

***

That night when I dreamt of him, there was no Jessica to wake me. Sean and I had spent hours talking and laughing, in the DVD shop. It wasn't until the manager had come over and told us it was closing time that I had noticed we were the only ones in there, which had made us laugh harder as we left the shop. I was still laughing when I woke up, and upon realising I had been dreaming, I was instantly sad. I didn't want to wake up.

In my dreams, I was a normal person. I didn't have a birthmark, and when Sean had looked at me, I'd felt like the most important person alive.

I did, however, have a slightly anxious feeling in my stomach. I'd actually spoken to him this time, certainly Jessica would find out. But right now I didn't care. I would deal with whatever she had waiting for me on Monday. In the meantime, I was happy. He wanted to see me again, even if it was to tell him how the film was, which I really did enjoy.

I got out of bed, and after I had used the bathroom, I got dressed and headed downstairs.

My parents were in the kitchen, the back door was open, the sun was shining brightly, and if I strained my ears, I could hear the birds singing.

"Morning." I chirped, as I placed two slices of bread in the toaster.

"Good morning!" My parents chorused.

"You sleep well?" My Mum asked, as she pulled one load of washing from the washing machine and put another load in.

"Like a baby." I smiled and started to hum as I pulled the butter and marmalade out of the cupboard. The look my parents gave each other didn't go unnoticed, but I chose to ignore it. "Kasey-Ray still in bed?"

"No, she's gone for a run." My Dad told me, as my Mum went to hang the washing out.

Kasey-Ray had been harping on about training for sports day, as she wanted to be on top form when she won. As far as she was concerned, she was going to come first in every event, and I had to say I agreed with her. I'd already known that Kasey-Ray was fast, but with her determination she could do anything.

"We're going for another walk later. Do you want to come?" I thought about this for a moment as I buttered my toast.

"Nah, I think I'm going to sunbathe." My Dad laughed. Normally this was something Kasey-Ray did.

"Okay." He replied, just as Kasey-Ray came in. She was all sweaty and out of breath as she walked to the sink to get a glass of water.

"What's happening?" She asked as she leant back against the sink to look at my Dad and me, as I went to sit at the kitchen table.

"Nothing much. Your Mum and I are going for a walk in a bit and Erin's going out back to sunbathe." He rolled his eyes at the last bit.

"Cool." She finished her water and rinsed her glass, placing it upside down on the draining board. "I'll grab a shower and come out and sunbathe with you." She said as she picked up my MP3 player and left the room. I'd wondered where it had gone, but I wasn't going to start screaming and shouting about it. I was still happy after speaking to Sean last night.

By the time I'd finished my breakfast my Mum had come in and was grabbing her handbag when she turned to me.

"When the machine is finished, hang it out please?" I nodded as I gave her a kiss."

"Will do." Then I carried my blanket outside to lie down. Not long after, Kasey-Ray came out, carrying a blanket under one arm, sun lotion in one hand, whilst using her free hand to hold her phone to her ear.

"No way! Really?" She said in shock as she tried to lay her blanket on the grass, "OH. MY. GOD!" She slowly and loudly spoke each word dramatically, as I took the blanket from her and laid it next to mine as she started to scream at an ear splitting volume.

After she hung up the phone she quickly dropped to the floor and she looked like she was ready to explode with excitement.

"Guess what?" She reached out and repeatedly shook my arm as she bounced up and down.

"What?" I tried to look interested.

"Matt likes me!" At first I was wondering who Matt was, then I remembered she'd pointed him out a couple of weeks ago. "Well Matt is friends with Jack and Jack is going out with Becca." I was started to get dizzy, trying to keep up. I had no idea who Jack or Becca was. "Well Claire just bumped into Becca and she was saying that Jack told her, that Matt likes me and is going to ask me out. Can you believe it?" I thought I was going to get a headache with information overload.

"Wow." Not because he was going to ask her out. I knew he would anyway. Mainly, wow, because I was still trying to sort all the information out in my head.

"I know! Isn't it amazing?" She smiled and clapped happily. She lay down on her blanket and started talking at supersonic speed, wondering when he would ask her out? Where he would ask her? Where he would take her? What she would wear? I lay there listening to her, drifting in and out of my own world. I imagined that I was Kasey-Ray and Matt was Sean. I would probably be acting the same way, if I'd just heard that Sean was interested. Not that it would ever happen, but a girl could dream. I sighed as I realised the washing machine had finished and went to get up.

"Where are you going?" Kasey-Ray interrupted my thoughts.

"I gotta hang out the rest of the washing for Mum."

I slowly took the washing out of the machine and by the time I went back outside, Kasey-Ray was back on her phone, talking to Claire again. I envied my sister; everything seemed so easy for her. All the other students hung on her every word. I didn't want to be like her in that way. I was used to being alone. It would just be nice to have maybe one friend and for someone like Sean, or rather Sean himself, be interested in me, without having to worry about what others thought.

How life would be different if I hadn't been born with this ugly birthmark. I didn't want to reverse roles with my sister. I just wished I had been born as perfect as her.

Chapter 5

On Monday, it was the same as the last. Jessica didn't acknowledge me again. I was beginning to feel excited at the prospect of seeing Sean on Friday. I could live with seeing him in secret. It was the closest thing to a real date I'd ever had, and probably would have.

I still saw him now and again, in the car park, but he never looked in my direction, or not that I was aware, because as soon as I looked in his direction I would quickly look away, not wanting to be caught out by Jessica.

By Friday, the teachers had stopped giving out homework, so as soon as I got home I ran straight upstairs to change out of my uniform. Every Friday I'd gone to the DVD rental shop in my school uniform and today I wanted to make an effort. I pulled on a pair of jeans, that was the easiest part, and then I turned to my drawers to find a top that I thought would make me half attractive.

After emptying nearly every drawer and wardrobe, I groaned in frustration as I found nothing to wear.

"We're leaving in a......" Kasey-Ray's voice trailed off as she found me sitting on the floor wearing just jeans and a bra, with nearly all my clothes scattered around the room. "You decorating or something?" She raised one eyebrow as she tried to make me laugh. It didn't work though. I was close to telling her I wasn't going anywhere.

"I can't find a top to wear." I huffed.

"Hmmm..." She raised both her eyebrows as she stared at me thoughtfully. "One sec." She turned and left the room, leaving me to wonder what she was doing. "Try this." She threw a purple top at me when she returned.

Standing up, I pulled it over my head and went to look in the mirror. It was a simple purple, long sleeved top with cuffs that flare out and buttons that started half way up. Smiling at my reflection, Kasey-Ray slipped a silver, sparkly belt around my waist.

"There you're perfect. The belt just added that little extra."

"Thank you so much." I turned to give her a huge hug.

"Now hurry up and do your hair," She flung my favourite silver headband at me, "I'll tell Mum and Dad you're on your way down."

She left me to adjust my hair. After I was happy that enough hair covered my birthmark, I pulled on my boots and hurried downstairs and out of the house, into the waiting car.

Kasey-Ray didn't say anything to me on the drive there. She just kept looking over at me, every so often, thoughtfully. I knew she would be watching me like a hawk tonight, and if he did turn up, she would probably interrogate me.

His car was already there when we arrived. Taking a deep breath, I slowly climbed out of the car, after a quick check of my appearance, under Kasey-Ray's quizzical eyes.

"Anything you want to tell me?" She pried as we walked through the shop's door, but my blushes spoke volumes, as I spotted him by the new releases. "Ahhhh!" Kasey-Ray nodded with understanding. "Is that him?" I'd never actually spoken about Sean. Kasey-Ray had heard through the school grapevine that Jessica was giving me a hard time over someone called Jacko. "He's hot." She added. I would have laughed, if I wasn't trying to steady my heart rate. "If you don't want him, I will have him." I glared at her as she raised her hands up and started to back away. Then with a nod towards Sean, she headed to where our parents were.

Smoothing down my clothes, I took another deep breath and walked towards him. He had his back to me, but I could see that he held a DVD in his hands, and I could just make out it was 'Four Lions'.

"Good choice." I stood next to him, purposely not making eye contact, as I casually pretended to look at the new releases.

"Hi." He smiled, making me turn to look at him. *Wow! He is gorgeous, better looking than any movie star or male model I've ever seen.* "You've seen it then?" He nodded at the DVD in his hand.

"Yep, watched it last week." I looked down at the DVD in his hands, because if I continued to stare into his eyes, I would probably faint.

"Did you not get the other DVD then?" He actually sounded disappointed.

"I did." I quickly reassured him. "My family and I get 3 or 4 DVD's a week."

"Wow, do you watch them all in one night?" I laughed at this, and never realised how weird it sounded, as rentals were only for one night.

"We try to." I exaggerated the word try. "But we have until seven the next day. Plus it's kind of a family tradition." Embarrassed that he may find me or my family strange.

"That's cool. My family are normally too busy for us all to sit down for more than an hour or two."

"That's a shame!" I didn't know what else to say, so I turned back to the DVD's, not that there was anything interesting here. I could happily spend eternity just watching his face. I wouldn't need to rent a DVD again.

"So was it good then?" He broke my thoughts making me blush.

"Sorry? Was what good?" I cringed thinking I'd missed something he'd said.

"Love and other drugs?"

"Yeah, I really enjoyed it" Nodding eagerly, I probably looked like one of those nodding dogs you found in people's cars.

"I may have to get it then" I wasn't sure if he was teasing or not, but before I could respond his phone went off. "I gotta go." He said pulling his phone from his pocket, whilst placing the DVD back on the shelf. "I'll see you next week?" He asked as he started to walk away. I nodded as he stopped to look back at me, "By the way," He paused as he looked outside then back to me, "You look really nice!"

"Th-thanks!" I stuttered as I blushed so red that you probably thought my whole face was covered by one giant birthmark.

He left then, without another word, as I watched him climb into his car. He raised his hand to wave as he pulled away, all the time I wanted to jump up and scream. *He had actually asked to see me next week. Oh my god, I can't believe it. The hottest boy on the planet wants to see me again.*

"Wow!" Kasey-Ray breathed out as she came to stand next to me. "I felt like a peeping tom watching you two." I nervously laughed, and then quickly changed the subject.

"Where's Mum and Dad?" I looked around to see them heading towards the counter. "Never mind, I see them. I'm going to wait outside; it's so hot in here." Through all my excitement I hadn't realised how hot I was. Kasey-Ray gave a full hearty laugh. "What's so funny?"

"Nothing." She followed me outside.

The night air hit my face with full force, making me feel dizzy as I reached over to steady myself on my sister.

"You okay?" All laughter gone now.

"Think so, I just feel dizzy." My head was spinning, I felt like I was burning up. I'd never felt like this before. I just needed to lie down for a bit.

"Erin love?" I heard the sound of my Mum's voice as she came to stand next to me, but before I could say anything I was sick. "Let's get you home."

Before I could argue my Dad had put me into the back of the car with my Mum, whilst Kasey-Ray climbed in front.

"We're going straight home, no pizza tonight." I knew he was talking to Kasey-Ray.

"Trust me!" Kasey-Ray started. "I don't want pizza after seeing that."

Luckily it was only a ten minute drive home. When we got there my Dad carried me up the stairs and put me on my bed.

"I'll sort her out," My Mum whispered to him. "Ask Kasey-Ray to bring me a bowl of cold water and a flannel please?"

I didn't know what was going on, I just felt extremely hot. I was aware of my Mum taking my clothes off, then I felt something cool press against my head, and then everything went black.

***

That was the first time I'd blacked out. I wasn't sure why I had been so ill, but when I woke up I felt fine. I looked around my darkened room, wondering where I was. The clock on my bedside table read 4:27am. I knew I needed the toilet, so I sat up and almost stood on someone sleeping on the floor.

"Oh sorry." I almost wet myself with fright when the person quickly got up.

"Oh, you're awake. How are you feeling?" It was my Mum and she sounded exhausted.

"Fine, I just need the toilet."

"Okay." She moved out of the way to let me past.

When I returned, she had switched on my lamp and was putting my quilt on my bed.

"Sorry about last night." I told her, but all she did was give me a weak smile. "Everything okay?" I asked, unsure by her reaction.

"Yes, it's just..." She paused for a moment and stood to look at me nervously, "it's Monday."

"You're joking?" *It must be a joke.* I sat on my bed in shock, but she shook her head. "Wow!" I reeled at the revelation, "I don't..." My voice trailed off, unable to find the right words.

"You had a fever and passed out." She told me very matter-of-factly. I'd never passed out before, but there again I'd never felt as hot as I did on Friday, but I felt fine now. I didn't understand.

"Have you been with me the whole time?"

"Pretty much." She nodded as she came to take my temperature. "You can stay off school today and the rest of the week."

"No. I want to go to school." I said as I went to find a clean uniform, "I only have three more days left!"

My Mum sighed as she realised she wasn't going to win this fight, and was probably too tired to even argue with me.

"Okay, but it's only 5am now." She picked up her pillow, putting it under her arm.

"I'm just going to have a shower and get dressed before breakfast. I'll probably watch TV downstairs, until Kasey-Ray is up."

"Okay!" My Mum yawned, "I'm going back to bed." Then she left me sorting out my uniform.

Once I was washed and dressed, I headed downstairs. I couldn't believe I'd slept the whole weekend away. I'd missed movie night.

After making some toast and a cup of tea, I carried them through to the living room to try and find something to watch on the TV. We had all these channels and do you think I could find anything to watch? Not a chance. Luckily there were a few good things starting at 6am. I thought I could watch one episode of Oprah, followed by Extreme Home Makeover.

By the time the last programme was finished I was in floods of tears, I heard the concerned shushing from my sister.

"No, I'm fine, honest," I said, wiping my tears as I looked at her, "I was just watching Extreme Makeover and you know how I get." I laughed through the tears.

"How can you cry when you got that hot old guy presenting it?" Kasey-Ray laughed as she tried to cheer me up, and it worked as my tears of sadness, turned to tears of joy.

"Trust you to make something sad end up being about a man." I laughed. "I can imagine, if I ever have an accident and need an ambulance, you'd be like 'stuff Erin, where are the hot paramedics'." I mimicked her as she tried to act offended.

"I'm just going to grab some breakfast, you had any?"

"Yeah! I grabbed some toast." I called after her.

It didn't take long for Kasey-Ray to finish her breakfast. Then we grabbed our bags and headed off to school. We didn't need our coats as the sun was shining brightly down on us.

"I can't believe I slept the whole weekend." I shook my head in disbelief. I don't think I'd ever slept longer than ten hours.

"You didn't miss much. We didn't even watch the DVD's we got." I was ready to start apologising when Kasey-Ray started laughing. "I wouldn't worry about it. Mum and Dad picked two DVD's and they both looked guff. You probably did me a favour." She was still laughing as we approached the school gates. "You okay now though?" She gave me a critical once over.

"Never better." I smiled hugely.

"One way to get out of the grilling I was going to give you." We both laughed as I realised she was talking about Friday night, and before she could start interrogating me, someone shouted her. We both looked to see it was Matt and he was standing with Claire. Saved again. She laughed as she waved at Claire and Matt. "I'll meet you after school."

"Okay." I watched as she almost bounced over to where her friends were waiting. I was sure I would hear all about this after school.

Just then I heard arguing, coming from the car park. The hairs on the back of my neck stood up as I recognised the voice. I wasn't sure exactly what was being said, but I was sure Jessica and Justin had had some kind of falling out, as she barged past me, almost knocking me over.

"Erin?" Kasey-Ray shouted over, obviously concerned for me, but I was fine. Jessica didn't seem mad at me, I just happened to be in her way. I wasn't the only one she had barged into.

Giving a weak smile and a wave, I pulled myself together and walked through the main doors.

Once I got to form room, Jessica was still mad. I heard her say some obscenities about Justin, but one thing was for sure, I would do whatever it took to stay out of her way today. I didn't want to be a punch-bag for her rage against Justin, and if she found out about my Friday nights, then I'm sure she would lose it.

"Is there a problem?" Ms Forrester had just walked through the door and stopped at Jessica's table.

"No Miss." She grunted.

"Well, if I ever hear you," She paused to look at everyone in the class, "Or anybody else, using that kind of language, you will be sent to Mr Jenkins office. Do I make myself clear?"

"Yes, Miss!" We all chorused.

Ms Forrester then headed to her table, pulled out the register and called our names.

Once form room was over, we all picked up our bags and started to leave.

"Not you, Jessica Watson."

Jessica stopped right in front of me and turned around. I froze. She looked right at me, but her eyes were glazed over, like she didn't register my existence, as she seemed to look right through me to Ms Forrester. I quickly stepped out of the way, letting her past, sure that if I hadn't, she would have pushed me out of the way. I thanked my lucky stars that I had no lessons with her today. I was scared to be in close proximity to her. It would only take the smallest thing to trigger Jessica. I felt sorry for anyone who got in her way today.

***

Today, everything went by quickly. Even at lunch time, when I sat outside to eat, it felt like I'd only just opened my lunch box when the bell rang.

There weren't really any lessons, per se. Mostly we played games, which made time go faster, and the other students actually spoke to me. Not really to make conversation, just because we were put into teams and had to talk. Either way, it was good to have other people to talk to. Most of the time the only conversations I had were with the teachers.

When the final bell rang, I quickly grabbed my bag and went to look for Kasey-Ray. I found her outside flirting with Matt.

"Hi." I said breezily, as I saw my sister blush. "Ready?"

"Give me a second!" She smiled as she turned back to Matt.

"Okay, I'll go sit on the wall." I slowly made my way to the wall next to the car park. I pulled a handmade fan out of my bag, that I had made it in one of my lessons. I started to wave it in front of my face, whilst closing my eyes.

"Someone's watching you." I heard Kasey-Ray coyly say.

"Eh?" I opened my eyes to look at my sister, but she was looking past me towards the car park, as I tried to follow her gaze she stopped me.

"Don't look." She put her hands to my face. "Jessica's there."

"Okay." As soon as she said her name, I quickly looked back at my sister. I watched her for a while as she continued to look past me towards the car park. "What's going on?" I could hear arguing and it took all my will power not to turn around and look.

"Jessica and the red headed guy are arguing."

"That's her boyfriend, Justin." I told her. Mainly so she could use his name and I wouldn't get confused. "Well, he is standing between her and Jacko. She's pointing at him and hurling abuse." She stopped me again, as I tried to turn around to see why. "Justin is dragging her away now." Kasey-Ray finally looked at me. "She's a fiery one, that one!" She tutted as she pulled me to my feet.

"Wonder why she was having a go at Sean?" I mainly asked to myself.

"Dunno. Maybe you can ask him on Friday!" She winked, making me laugh even though I was still nervous and worried. Maybe she'd found out about the Friday nights. Tomorrow I was sure I would feel her wrath and would probably not see Sean on Friday. The sense of disappointment washed over me, making me feel sick at the thought of not talking to him again.

"Anyway," Kasey-Ray breezed, itching to change the subject, "Matt asked me out." She squealed as she squeezed my arm. "He wants to take me out on Wednesday night." She crooned. She was acting like she'd won the lottery.

"Where's he taking you?"

"Bowling and here's the thing."

"Uh-oh." There always had to be something with Kasey-Ray, something that would involve me covering for her.

"Well, there isn't a bowling alley near here, so we would get back late. Ooooo..." She smiled at me, "Claire suggested she could tag along and Matt could bring Liam, mainly cos she fancies him." She laughed as she rolled her eyes, "and then afterwards I can sleep over at Claire's." She smiled like it was a perfect plan.

Kasey-Ray and I both had a curfew of 10pm, which even I thought was reasonable. I couldn't even imagine how late she would arrive back.

"Claire's going to ask her Mum when she gets home and call me. Her Mum's pretty laid back, so she reckons it'll be fine."

I didn't know much about Claire. I just knew she was an only child to a single Mum.

"So where do I fit into all of this?" She hadn't actually said she wanted my help, but I knew I was involved somewhere.

"If Mum and Dad ask, don't mention bowling or Matt. Please?" double close quote mark She dragged the last word out as she gave me her puppy dog eyes. Sighing I gave her a serious expression. I hated lying, especially to our parents. "Look, hopefully they won't say or ask you anything, so you won't have to lie." She moved to stand in front of me. "Please sis?" She begged. "I promise I won't ask you to do anything like this again." I laughed at this statement, because even though she meant every word she had said, I knew there would be a next time.

"Okay!" I sighed.

"Yay!" She picked me up in a bear hug and swung me around.

"You owe me." I raised an eyebrow. "Big time. If you get found out and they knew I was covering for you."

"They won't." She assured me, she took my arm again as we turned into our street.

Chapter 6

Claire had called later that evening. She had apparently told her Mum everything and she had agreed to let Kasey-Ray sleep over. I was actually surprised how quickly my parents had agreed to let her sleep out. None of us had actually slept over at a friend's house before. Not as if I ever would. I needed to have friends to sleep over at.

All I needed now was for my parents to find out and all hell would break loose.

"I promise they won't find out." Kasey-Ray tried to reassure me on the way to school. "It's fool-proof and they don't even know Claire's Mum, and if they need to get hold of me, I have my mobile." She said as she pulled her phone out of her bag and waved it in front of my face.

I could understand her reasoning. I was just a worrier. I sighed as I pushed her hand away from the front of my face.

"Just don't slip up." I raised my finger to her, as she laughed. "It's not funny. I know how excited you get and then you have a habit of rabbiting on too much." Kasey-Ray had stopped again to pretend she was locking her mouth shut and throwing away the key.

"I promise." She then crossed her heart. Seeing the defeated expression in my face she gave me a huge hug, "You're the best sister ever!"

"Kasey-Ray!" Claire shouted, making my sister jump around.

"Gotta go." She gave me another hug. "See you this afternoon and you better be cheering the loudest." She winked.

"Of course."

Today was sport's day. Whilst most of the students had to spend the morning going to lessons, all the students who were not taking part in any of the events, including myself, had to help setting up for each event and all the stalls.

The first part of the morning, I had to help put out all the chairs for the students, and then separate them by year, then by forms by coloured ribbon with the names of each form and year on them.

After break, we set up each of the events and stalls. When lunch time arrived, there were still things left to do, so in between eating my lunch, I was back and forth doing the final touches, along with a few fellow students.

"Well done." Ms Forrester said to me, as she appeared at the programme stall we would be working on. I had about fifteen minutes left before the rest of the school would start appearing. Their families had already started making their way over.

"I'm just going to bring our form room over." She told me, after a final check of the stall. "Will you be okay?"

"Yeah, it should be a breeze." I smiled nervously. There were going to be hundreds of people milling around the stalls and it was intimidating. With a smile, Ms Forrester quickly hurried off.

Luckily, I didn't have time to stay nervous once people started appearing at my stall. Most didn't even look at me as they handed me the money and I handed them a programme. I hadn't actually realised there was a queue forming until Ms Forrester appeared and started ordering people into 2 lines.

"Hi love," My Mum appeared at the front of my queue, "You look run off your feet."

"You could say that." I flushed. I barely had time to properly look at her and felt bad for rushing her to one side.

"I'll leave you to it. Come find me when you're done." My Mum touched my hand then went off to find a place to stand and watch.

"Nearly done," Ms Forrester blew out a sigh of relief, as I looked up to see the queue had dwindled down to about ten people. "After we've done those, why don't you go have a half hour break." She smiled, which was great, as I wanted to go find my Mum and at least try to watch one of races my sister was in.

Leaving my rucksack behind the stall with Ms Forrester, I picked up my drink and headed off to find my Mum. It didn't take me long to find her. She was talking to my sister as she stood with the rest of her form.

"Hi," I said breathlessly, as I went to stand next to them.

"Great timing." She hugged me with excitement. "They are just about to call all the 800 metre competitors. The 1500 has just finished." No sooner had she said this when Mr Jenkins's voice announced that all the 800 metre competitors should start making their way to the inside of the track.

"Break a leg!" I called after her. "Shall we try and find a better place to stand?" I asked my Mum, as we linked arms.

"I was just thinking the same thing." She kissed the side of my head.

We made our way through the crowd whilst the year one race started. By the time we'd found a spot, at one end of the track near the finish line, year two had just started.

We spotted Kasey-Ray warming up. She didn't look even a tiny bit nervous.

"Is Dad coming?" I asked, hoping that he would see at least one of the race's Kasey-Ray was competing in.

"Yeah, he should be on his way." She told me, as she looked at her watch.

"I'm going to have to head back after she's raced this." I pointed towards my sister as I saw her lining up.

She was off as soon as the starting pistol fired. I was jumping up and down, whilst clapping my hands and shouting my sister's name. For the first 600 metres she was neck and neck with Sophie, then at the final 200 metres she started breaking away. I could see Sophie digging hard, trying to keep up with my sister, but no matter how hard she tried Kasey-Ray just pulled away further. When she finally crossed the finish line in first place, my Mum and I were hugging and we could hear her form room cheering loudly. You could see the hope radiate through them, maybe this year, they would take first place.

Kasey-Ray seemed to put her all into the race and I knew she would do it for every race to come. But what I loved about Kasey-Ray was that she didn't gloat. As soon as Sophie crossed the line, she went straight over to give her a hug. I did hope that Sophie didn't take losing too hard. So many people out there, who are used to coming first in everything they do, don't like it when they are no longer known as the best. They should realise that it is the taking part that counts and that even though they may not be the best at something, they are doing their best and that is a great sense of achievement in itself. It is better than going to bed thinking of what ifs.

Kasey-Ray spotted my Mum and me, after scanning all the spectators, and waved as she made her way back to her seating area.

"I gotta go!" I kissed my Mum. "Hopefully I'll get to watch her win another." I didn't really care if she won another race. I just felt a sense of pride as I thought *that's my sister,* and I loved her so much. I stroked the necklace that she had given me for my birthday. I wore it constantly. I was proud to call her my sister.

There wasn't much to do, when I got back to the stall, where Ms Forrester was putting the last of the programmes on the table.

"Welcome back," She smiled up at me. "Are you okay whilst I go check on our form?" I nodded, I didn't need asking.

After putting the majority of the money that we'd collected from selling the programmes, inside a large canvas money bag, she carried it off with her.

"I'll be back soon." She gave me a quick smile and disappeared into the crowd.

"Can I have one of those please?" A girl's voice pulled me back to the stall. At first I didn't recognise who she was, as she handed me £2. She wore a friendly smile as I took her money and handed her a programme. Then I saw the twins standing behind her, looking in opposite directions. "Thanks Erin!" I blushed when she emphasised my name. Then she turned away with her hair flipping behind her, the purple and blue stripes dazzling in the sunlight.

Wow! She knows my name. I sat down on one of the chairs behind the stall. *I wonder if she knows about me bumping into her brother every Friday night?* I wasn't sure. I was surprised that she even knew my name.

"Erin," Ms Forrester appeared next to me. "I think I can handle the rest of this now. You go and enjoy yourself and watch your sister. I hear she just won the 200 metres." I wanted to squeal with delight when she told me this. I was also disappointed that I had missed it. "If you hurry, you'll catch her running the next race." She said as she picked up my rucksack and handed it to me.

"Thanks Miss!"

"No. Thank you!" She smiled, "I'll see you tomorrow."

I really like Ms Forrester. From day one she'd never judged me. She saw past my birthmark and saw me as the person, deep down, I felt I was.

I quickly hurried through the crowds to where I'd left my Mum. Now my Dad was standing next to her. I had just stood next to them when Kasey-Ray started her race, not giving me enough time to say hello to my Dad, as I jumped up and down. Again my sister came first, but only just. Later I was to be told that it was by 0.4 seconds.

It was her final race and her form were cheering wildly, sure they had finally won this year, but they would have to wait until all the events had finished and points added up.

Just as Kasey-Ray walked off the track and before we walked round to congratulate her, I was able to watch Jessica win her race, and by a large margin too. Our form didn't seem to cheer as loudly as Kasey-Ray's had. Maybe it was because they were used to her winning and I was sure that if she and Kasey-Ray were to race, that she would leave my sister standing. What was scary was that even though Jessica had won by such a large margin, it didn't look like she was even trying. I shivered at the thought as my Dad put his arm around my shoulder to steer me towards my sister.

"Hi Dad."

"Hi sweetie," he kissed the top of my head. "You been busy?"

"It's been non-stop." I nodded, but I hadn't felt like today was a chore. I would probably enjoy doing this every day, rather than doing lessons.

"Dad!" Kasey-Ray shouted excitedly. "Did you see me?" She looked like she was waiting for him to say no, disappointment ready to make her cry.

"Of course sweetie. I got here to see you do the 200 metres." He leaned forward to kiss my sister.

"Everyone reckons our form has won." She looked like she thought so too.

"Well how about we get take-out to celebrate?" He asked.

"Chinese?" She beamed as he nodded "Yay!"

Just then Mr Jenkins announced he would be starting to call the names of those students who came first and that they should come up to the stand in the centre of the track to collect their certificates. He slowly called the names of the students from year one, followed by each year after that. I did notice that Jessica had won a total of 7 events. I don't think I'd ever seen one person win so many.

Once all the students had received all of their individual certificates, it was time to announce which forms had won.

"After I have announced which form has won the trophy and name plaque, I would like that year to carry their chairs into the sports hall and back to your form rooms." His voice boomed loudly over the speakers. "Please do this in an orderly fashion and do it quietly."

Then he announced the year one winning form, then the second. We all stood there, nervously, as year two carried their chairs, as we waited for Mr Jenkins to announce Kasey-Ray's year.

When he finally did announce the form that had won, there was confusion at first. It was tied, and all was quiet. Kasey-Ray was the first to start clapping and cheering. Their form had finally won. Even though it was shared by two forms, Kasey-Ray's form had never won before, so that was a victory in itself. They would get their name on a plaque, outside Mr Jenkins's office. There was still only one trophy, so it would be shared by each of the form rooms, taking it in weekly turns.

There was no surprise when it was announced that my form had won. I lightly clapped my hands, but not as enthusiastically as I did when Kasey-Ray's form had won.

That night exuded happiness and excitement. We had our take-out and when it was time for bed, I was beaming. I'd never felt so happy and proud of my family, as I did right then.

Chapter 7

It was the last day of school, before the summer holiday. Kasey-Ray was going to Claire's house straight from school. She'd told our parents that Claire was having a sleepover. She had just failed to mention that she and Claire had dates that night. She'd told me earlier in the week that Matt Whitburn, a year five student, had asked her out. I had known she liked him and I knew it wouldn't take long before he found out too.

School had gone quickly. We spent the whole day in our form room playing games. We had been told we could bring in games from home. I had decided to just bring in my Nintendo DS, as I knew the rest of the students wouldn't invite me to play any of their games.

There was a buzz in the air after sports day, the day before. Each winning form had been taken up to reception to have a group photograph next to it. I didn't really see why I should be in the picture; I didn't compete in any of the events.

Either way, I was so glad when it was time to go home, I could relax and not worry about what other people were thinking, or whether Jessica had found out about my meet-ups with Sean or not.

I walked through the school gates and headed home. I was about half way, when I spotted them. Sat in the black Fiat Punto, were Sean, Paul and James, with Kelly in the driver's seat. A few steps away I spotted Justin and Jessica, who seemed to be having a heated argument. Mainly one sided. Jessica's red hair seemed to blow fiercely around her, even though there was no wind.

I stopped and paused for a moment, unsure whether to continue walking or not. Jessica hadn't bothered me for a while now, but that still didn't stop me from feeling on edge every time I saw her, especially when she was so angry.

I looked to the field on my right. I could easily climb the fence, walk across the field, through the trees at the far end. It should bring me out two streets away from my home. I hadn't noticed that it had gone quiet and they were all watching me.

I looked over at their faces, and for some reason they all looked nervous. Then my eyes fell on Jessica. She was furious.

"I warned you!" She seethed. I could see her slowly moving towards me. Her teeth grinding together and her hands were clenching and unclenching in fists.

My heart started to beat faster, my palms became sweaty. It was hard to swallow, with the huge lump that had appeared in my throat.

"Jess!" I saw Justin place his hands on her arms. "It's not time." I think I heard him say, as I saw movement from the car and the others started to get out.

Jessica had noticed too, making her start running towards me.

In that second I knew I had to jump the fence. I dropped my rucksack and hurtled over the fence, throwing myself into a sprint across the field. But it was too late. She was too fast.

I felt like my head was being pulled off. I screamed as she dragged me to the ground and started kicking and punching me. I was sure one of my ribs broke. The pain was excruciatingly unbearable. I couldn't stop screaming.

Why was no one helping me? Why had no one got her off me? Why me? What had I done? Why? Why? Why?

I started to feel angry. The feeling of heat from my anger was building and building to the point where it took over the pain. I couldn't control it. I'd never felt so angry before. That's when I heard Jessica scream.

"She's burnt me!" Jessica yelped both in pain and confusion.

"There's a towel and a couple of bottles of water in the back of the car." I heard Kelly say. "Paul? James? You go get them. Justin?" She paused for a moment. I was still curled up in a ball. I had no idea what was going on. *Who burnt who?* All I knew was my anger was starting to fade and the pain was taking over. Tears streamed down my face. I still couldn't look up when Kelly continued. "Get her out of here!" she snapped.

I expected to feel hands on me, dragging me up, but I felt nothing. It sounded like I was alone. All I could hear were my muffled cries of pain.

"Erin?" I heard the concerned voice of Sean whisper in my ear.

I didn't move or speak. I started to take deep breaths to try and overcome the pain.

"Can you hear me Erin?" Kelly asked in a soothing voice.

Then I felt someone stroking my left cheek. I froze. Was my mind playing tricks on me? My breathing started to accelerate and the stroking stopped, but the hand didn't move off my cheek.

"Shhh, it's okay, we won't hurt you." It was Sean again. It must have been his hands on my cheek. He went back to stroking my face as I heard footsteps approaching.

"We phoned Kate, and she's going to meet us at the cottage." I heard Paul and James chorus.

"Erin?" Kelly spoke this time. She didn't wait for a reply. "I'm just going to put some water on you and wrap you in a towel." She told me gently, as I curled up tighter in a frightened ball.

I couldn't feel water on me, just the sound of something hissing. I did start to feel cooler though, which was a plus, but the pain was still there and taking control of my body.

I didn't even want to look down to examine myself. If I was in this much pain, I could only imagine how bad I looked.

Suddenly I felt someone put a towel around me and lift me up into their arms, in one quick movement.

Before I could open my eyes or try and get away, everything went black.

***

I wasn't sure what had happened next, how I got here, or even where I was. I could just hear voices around me whispering heatedly. I was sure I recognised my parents, but I couldn't be certain.

What I was aware of was that I was lying in someone's arms. Their shirt was open and my head was pressed against their chest. I could hear the rhythmic beating of their heart. But what I really noticed was their hand stroking my left cheek.

It felt like I was dreaming. Not in a million years would I be lying here in a boy's arms. The only man's arms I'd ever laid in were my Dad's.

I slowly opened my eyes and peered through my lashes. I was in a room made purely of stone blocks. There was an unlit fire place next to me, with a shelf above it that held candles and picture frames. I couldn't make out who were in the pictures, but there was something familiar about them. I was sure I'd seen them before.

My eyes continued to search the room. I'd made the conscious decision not to move my head yet. Along one wall stood a giant bookcase, full of old books I'd never seen before.

I could still hear voices coming from somewhere behind me. Now I was more than positive that my parents were there, as I heard my Mum's furious voice saying something about Justin and how he should train his pets better.

Slowly, I tried to move my head up.

"Hi." Sean whispered gently. I could feel his warm breath on top of my head. I managed to slowly pull my head up to meet his gaze.

His eyes were full of concern. I couldn't believe my face was so close to his. His eyelashes were so long, and his eyes so deep and tranquil.

I could feel and smell his breath on me. I couldn't quite tell what it smelt of, but it was delicious. His lips were evenly proportioned, covering his perfect teeth. It would take me less than a second to press my lips to his.

"Sorry," was all I could I could get out. Mainly for what I was just thinking, but also because he'd had to put up with me in his arms.

It hurt to talk, and I tried to adjust my body into a sitting position, then winced and gasped in pain.

"Erin?" Before I could blink, my parents were on the floor, at my feet, with faces full of concern.

"Hi!" I croaked and without thinking I rested back against Sean's chest. I still didn't know why his shirt was open, but, right now, I didn't care. It felt warm, and safe.

His hand still remained on my face. Though now he had stopped stroking it. I felt his cheek rest on the top of my head, and I was sure his lips just brushed by hair, but I couldn't be sure. Everything felt so surreal.

"How are you feeling?" My Mum's voice worried asked, as her hands stroked my leg.

"Sore." My bottom lip trembled as I started to remember why I was in so much pain. Tears started to fill my eyes.

"Shhh!" My Dad soothed. "It's ok. You're safe now. She's not here and she won't get anywhere near you."

Just hearing him mention her, without even saying her name, made me anxious and scared. Tears started to roll down my cheeks and Sean's smooth fingers gently brushed them away and resumed stroking my left cheek again.

It was comforting. I had no idea why he was still here, why I was still in his arms, why he hadn't run off and left me? Why would someone as perfect as him want to be so close to someone like me?

Yes, my parents had always told me that I was special and unique. That God had left his mark of love on my left cheek, because he thought I was special too.

No matter how many questions I had, I didn't want to leave his warm, comforting embrace. It felt like his arms were made just for me.

"It's ready." Kelly spoke, interrupting my thoughts.

Why was she still here? And what was ready?

"Thanks." My Mum replied, then turned back to face me. "Erin?" She was now standing and had her arms out, reaching for me.

Before I could respond, Sean had stood up, with me in his arms.

"I'll carry her through, if that's okay?" It wasn't really a question, and I saw my parent's exchange a glance.

Sean, seeing the panic in my eyes tilted his head forward to whisper in my ear.

"It's okay. You're safe. I'm not going to let anyone hurt you. I'll be right here when you get back."

Back from where?

I think the alarm in my eyes had asked the question.

"Don't worry." He then kissed the top of my head. This startled me. He saw this and smiled. I could have stayed like this forever. This was probably what heaven felt like, apart from the pain in my ribs that hurt every time I took a breath. But something broke my thoughts, or rather a smell. It smelled like lots of flowers and fruit. I could only pick out the smell of Lavender and Oranges.

My Mum was already two steps ahead and had already opened the door to where the wonderful smells were coming from. Then I realised we were in a bathroom. Not too big, it fitted a bath and sink on one wall and a toilet on another.

Sean gently placed me down on the floor. It hurt to stand, so I leaned into him for support. He didn't seem to mind, but my Mum did.

"You'll need to leave now!" She told him sternly, making me panic. I didn't want him to leave. He said he would stay with me.

Before the rantings in my head got the better of me, Sean stroked the left side of my face with the back of his hand.

"I'll be in the other room." he smiled reassuringly.

Once he'd left the room and shut the door behind him, my Mum helped me take my clothes off. I gasped when I saw all the deep purple bruises. Some were raised and some had broken skin, with dry blood surrounding them. Some had dried to my clothes and I cried out in pain as my Mum pulled my fabric out of the already dried wounds. Where I'd been kicked and stamped in the ribs, there seemed to be a footprint. My body shook as I saw myself naked. How could anyone do this to a person?

My clothes were ruined. My Mum had told me that she was going to have to throw them in the bin.

She eased me slowly into the bath. I couldn't remember the last time she had seen me naked, let alone put me in the bath. She placed a bath pillow carefully behind my head, whilst I watched her face. She looked like she wanted to cry, but she was putting on a brave face for me.

"Where are we?" My voice was no louder than a whisper, "And why are we here?" I had so many questions I wanted to ask. But I didn't want to ask her the main questions, which were all about Sean. Why wasn't he repulsed by me?

My parents hated it when I spoke negatively about myself. So I knew this type of question would just upset her more.

"We are at your grandparent's cottage." She stood up straight and went to light some incense sticks that were on the window-sill. "But there's no need to worry yourself with trivial questions right now." She turned back to me and smiled. But all I could do was think about Jessica. I tried to sit up in a panic and ended up crying out. "Hey, hey!" she soothed. "You're fine. We will answer any questions in due time." She leaned over to kiss my forehead. "I'll be back shortly. Just lie back and try to relax." Before I could reply she was gone.

I'm not sure how long I lay there for. Fifteen minutes? Thirty? An hour? Too long, in my opinion. I had let my mind run over things that had happened today. *Where was Jessica now?*

I didn't hear my Mum return. I was too deep in my own thoughts. I jumped when she touched my arm. She smiled at the confused look in my face. *Why hadn't it hurt when I moved?* Actually, I didn't feel any pain. I looked across my body to examine my bruises, which were deep purple when I'd gotten into the bath. Now they were a yellowy brown colour.

"It's the medicine in the bath." She answered my unspoken question, as she laid what looked like some clothes on top of the closed toilet seat and opened a large bath sheet and hung it over the radiator. "I've brought you some pyjamas and I've called Kasey-Ray and told her where we are and that we'll collect her tomorrow evening." She turned back to me thoughtfully. "When you've finished, just get out and get dressed. I'll be in the other room. I'll have a mug of hot chocolate waiting for you."

Without waiting for a reply, she smiled at my opened mouth expression, and left the room.

Reaching for the soap, I started to wash myself. I couldn't believe I felt no pain. When I was finished, I climbed out of the bath and wrapped myself in the towel. It was so warm and soft.

I walked across to where the clothes lay, to examine them more closely with a feeling of dread. I hoped my Mum hadn't brought my favourite pyjamas, which were too short in the legs and full of holes. The sense of relief filled me when I realised she hadn't, as I picked up a pair of pink satin pyjama's, which I hadn't seen before, let alone worn.

I slowly dressed and brushed my hair, without looking in the mirror. Then I sat on the closed toilet lid, chewing my fingernails, I sat there for at least five minutes, trying to build up the courage to go into the next room. Taking a deep breath, I stood up and took the five steps from the toilet to the door and placed my hand on the door handle.

I could hear different conversations, but I couldn't make out what was being said. I think my Dad must have told a joke because I heard Paul and James laugh in unison.

With another deep breath I turned the handle and opened the door.

Everyone turned to look at me, which made me feel self-conscious. I was used to people staring, but not with smiles on their faces.

The fire was lit. It smelled wonderful and the sound was so relaxing. On the floor were the twins and Kelly. The twins seemed to be hanging on every word my Dad said, who sat on the seat next to my Mum on an old two seater sofa. My Mum and Kelly were talking about... cooking, I think.

Sitting alone in the armchair that Sean and I had sat in, facing the fire, was Justin. He wasn't smiling. In fact, he looked depressed, like he had the weight of the world on his shoulders.

In the middle, facing directly to the fire, was a three-seater sofa. On one end, making me gasp as I took in how even more beautiful Sean was, with the colours of the fire reflecting off his face.

How could one person get better looking every time I saw them?

He was smiling a huge smile, which made his eyes dance and my heart flutter. He patted the seat next to him and held out his hand. I hesitated for a moment, not completely sure what to do. Everyone else had gone back to their conversations. So taking a deep breath to slow my racing heart, I took the eleven steps over to where he sat.

He pulled me down next to him and gently put his arm around my shoulders before reaching over to grab a mug of hot chocolate from the table next to him and handed it to me.

Then without warning, he pulled me close and kissed my forehead. Instead of releasing me, he kept me pressed against him as I drank my hot chocolate. I was aware of the feeling of him burying his head into my damp hair. *What was going on here?* I wanted to shout.

"You smell nice." He murmured into my hair.

I didn't reply. I was too confused with what was happening, so I just sat and drank my hot chocolate.

When I was finished, he took the empty mug from my hands and placed it back on the table, then he reached back with his free hand and placed it on mine. Without realising, he had moved the hand that was furthest away from him, and placed it around his waist, like I was embracing him. I wasn't complaining. I was confused.

"Tired?" He asked, moving his head to look into my eyes.

I quickly shook my head, not wanting to admit that I was shattered.

My eyes glanced across his shirt, to see if it was still open. Unfortunately, it wasn't. I sighed, I knew I must be dreaming and eventually I would wake up. Then I felt his fingers gently stroking my left cheek. My body started to relax, my eyes grew heavy and I fought with them to stay open. I knew that if they closed and I opened them again I would be in my own bed and none of this would have happened.

I couldn't fight it anymore and eventually my eyes closed.

***

I woke to the sound of birds singing and the smell of bacon cooking. My eyes were still closed, but it felt like I was in my own bed, cuddled up to my duvet, which was pressed against my bedroom wall.

Damn, I knew it was a dream.

Then my duvet seemed to shake and a quiet laugh escaped from it. My eyes flew open and I saw that my face was nestled against a man's chest. I jumped and nearly fell off where ever I was lying, but his arm caught me protectively.

"Hi sleepy!" Sean smiled widely as he leaned down to kiss my head.

We were still on the sofa. He lay against the back, propped up on one arm with my whole body pressed against his.

"Hi." I smiled shyly, putting my hand over my mouth, so he wouldn't smell my morning breath.

"Hungry sweetheart?" I heard my Dad ask from behind me.

I wanted to turn around and reply, but I didn't want to move. My Dad sensed this and appeared behind the back of the sofa, just next to Sean's head.

"Uh-huh!" I replied, still keeping my hand tightly over my mouth.

"Okay, I'll go tell your Mum that you're awake and hungry."

Then he disappeared, leaving my heart racing, as Sean lowered his head to the pillow we were sharing.

"You sleep well?" He gazed into my eyes with pure adoration. *What the heck was going on here?*

I nodded, and he smiled sweetly at me.

We lay like that for a long time, neither of us saying a word or looking away. It was my Mum who broke my gaze, by leaning over the sofa to inform me that breakfast was ready. All the time Sean continued to watch my face. It was like he was studying it. Cramming all the information he could get from my face for some big test.

He only broke his gaze when I tried to move. Then he adjusted his body, so he could help me up.

As he helped me to a standing position, I felt his hand slide, slowly and gently, down my back, instantly sending shivers up and down my spine.

"Did you bring my toiletry bag over?" I called to either of my parents.

"Your Dad's just left to go get it and pick you up some fresh clothes." My Mum called from the kitchen. "He'll be back by the time you finish your breakfast."

"Okay!" I sighed. I really did want to brush my teeth before I ate.

Still, I could go and see if there was any toothpaste in the bathroom that I could put on my finger and run around my mouth.

I walked into the bathroom and closed the door behind me, sighing when I realised there was no lock on the door.

After I'd finished using the toilet, I walked over to the sink, to look for the toothpaste. Just as I started, I caught a glimpse of myself in the bathroom cabinet.

"Mum?" I called in my normal voice. "Mum?" I called again, louder and more urgently. I was about to call her again when she burst through the door.

She stood with her back to the closed door, watching me carefully, as I looked away from her and back to my reflection in the mirror.

Slowly I raised my hand to my left cheek and stroked it. I looked back at my Mum with questions in my eyes, and then turned back to my reflection.

My birthmark was still there, but it seemed to have shrunk and faded.

"What's happening?" I asked with tears welling up in my eyes. I wasn't sure why I was crying. I'd always wished it would disappear, but I had never expected it.

Turning to face my Mum, she looked like she was trying to find the right words.

"Tell me!" I almost screamed at her, taking a step towards her, and it hurt and confused me when she stepped back. "Mum?"

She went to turn and reach for the door handle and this infuriated me. What was she hiding?

Before I could reach out to grab hold of her, she was gone.

"Mum!" I shouted angrily, as I went to follow her.

By the time I'd left the bathroom, my Mum was standing behind Sean. I wasn't sure where the others were. Then I heard my Mum speak quietly to Sean, like she was hoping I wouldn't hear.

"Sean, do something."

"Do something?" I yelled. "What the hell is going on? Why are you acting like you are scared of me? I don't understand. I don't even know why Sean is here!" I screamed as I pointed at him. "I want to know what's happening? Why...." My voice trailed off as I went to reach up to touch my left cheek and I saw that flames were covering my arms.

I screamed and started waving my arms frantically; causing me fall to the ground, as I noticed the rest of my body was on fire too.

I didn't feel like I was on fire. I just felt scared.

Out of the corner of my eye and through my screaming, I saw Sean quickly approach me and reach his hand to my face.

Why wasn't he catching fire?

"I don't want to die." I cried hysterically.

He didn't look scared. He just looked concerned. He touched my left cheek and started stroking. This calmed me slightly, and before I had a chance to do, feel or say anything, he had pulled me into his arms and stayed there with me on the floor, rocking me back and forth, whilst resting his face on top of my head and stroking my left cheek.

I was unsure how long we stayed like that before I stopped crying and pulled away from him to look at my arms. I couldn't see any traces of them having been on fire. I started to touch his chest and check his arms, and he was still as perfect as ever.

Tears started to fill my eyes again.

"What's going on?" I looked up to his face and pleaded with him. "Am I losing my mind?" The last word caught in my throat, as tears trickled down my face.

He shook his head and before I could look back down he placed a finger under my chin and stared into my eyes, intently.

"No, you're not losing your mind."

"What's happening to me?" My face crumpled and I moved my head down and buried it into his chest.

"You're my fire goddess." He whispered in a serious tone.

I pulled away and stared at him in disbelief.

He didn't look like he was joking. I was ready to start shouting at him, when he put his fingers to my lips, stopping me from speaking.

Eventually, when he knew I wasn't going to say another word, he moved his hand and eyes to my left cheek and stared thoughtfully at my birthmark.

Without saying a word, he cupped my face in his hands and leaned his face closer to kiss my birthmark. By the time he pulled away, my eyes were closed. He waited until I opened them before he spoke.

"I can't explain it fully." He placed a finger to my lips again, stopping my attempt to talk. "But this is what I do know." He removed his finger from my lips and placed it back on my birthmark, "when you manage to completely control this!" His other hand stroked my arms as his other finger gently lifted off my birthmark and then placed it back again. "Then this will disappear."

I shook my head and moved away from him, as I scrambled to my feet before he could stop me from talking.

"So the fire is real?" I started to pace the room. By now, my Mum had left. Sean nodded as he slowly got to his feet and went to reach out for me. "Don't!" I growled, stepping out of his reach. "What are you doing here?" I pointed at him as he flinched. This hurt him, but I didn't stop. "You could have any girl in Galladale, probably any girl out of Galladale too, but instead you decide to hang around with a monster! I just don't get it." It was my turn to put my finger to his lips. "What's even going on here?" Removing my finger to point from him to me.

I knew I was probably being stupid. Here was this gorgeous guy, who seemed to want to be with me, and now I was rejecting him. But how could I continue to move forward with anything in my life, when I didn't even know what was happening to me.

Sean sighed and stepped forward. This time I didn't move away and stayed frozen as he reached for my hand.

He raised my hand to his cheek. I hadn't noticed that flames were coming from my hands. As my hand touched his face, the flames fizzled out.

He left my hand on his cheek, as he slowly moved his hand up my arm, from my wrist to my shoulder. As his hand moved over my body, the flames dispersed.

"W-w-w-what a-a-are y-y-youuu?" I stuttered.

He didn't answer me. He just slowly stepped closer, until eventually I was in his arms.

Without another word, he leaned down and gently kissed my lips.

When he pulled away he reached his hands to my cheeks.

"You are not a monster!" He paused to look at me, before he continued. "And I don't want just any girl. I want you!" I was about to say something when he kissed me again. When he moved away, he placed a finger back to my lips. "I've always wanted you, and as corny as it may sound, you complete me." He paused for a moment, like he was trying to find the right words. "And in answer to your question, I can only tell you the basics. I am sure Dr Hammersmith can explain in more detail when he gets here later."

He didn't let me interrupt as he continued talking, like I knew exactly who Dr Hammersmith was and that he was coming.

"You are my fire and I am your water!"

This comment actually made more sense than it should have.

We stood there in silence for a long time, just staring into each other's eyes.

"Come on, let's go get something to eat." He said as he pulled me towards the kitchen.

Chapter 8

As we walked into the kitchen, my Dad was standing looking out of the window, with a cup in his hands.

"Hi sweetie," He smiled my favourite smile.

"Hey Dad!" I slowly walked towards him and gave him a hug. He hugged me back so tightly I thought I was going to burst. Realising this, he quickly released me and stepped back to examine me.

"Sorry sweetie, I don't know my own strength half the time." He smiled at me weakly. "You should eat something."

I hadn't actually realised how hungry I was until he said that and my stomach growled in reply, making me laugh.

My Dad turned to grab two plates of full English breakfast and placed them on the kitchen table, in front of Sean and me. "Where's Mum?" I enquired with my mouth full of egg and bacon.

"Gone for a walk." My Dad replied as he sat down at the table with his cup in his hands.

We sat in silence for a while as Sean and I continued to eat.

"I'm sorry your Mum and I didn't explain things sooner." I continued to eat as I listened to what my Dad had to say. "You see we had hoped it would skip a generation, but you started to show sign's early on."

My hand gripped my knife tightly, as Sean placed his hand on top of mine and stroked it gently.

My Dad didn't seem to notice this, or refused to acknowledge my discomfort.

"From birth we knew you were special. Your birthmark was always hotter than the rest of your body, and when you were upset, it would burn fiercely."

He stood up from his seat and walked towards the kitchen sink to stare out the window thoughtfully for a moment or two.

When he turned back his face was suddenly very serious.

"Your Mum and I were also born with unique gifts, like you and Sean." He nodded to each of us as he said our names. "I possess the ability to make thunder." He looked back out the window, "and your Mum can make lightening." He turned back to face us again and walked towards the table. "You see alone we are dangerous and powerless to control our abilities. But together..."

"Together, we are powerful and have the most calming effect on the other." My Mum finished my Dad's sentence as she came to stand next to him and smiled at me apologetically mouthing 'sorry to' me.

I stood up from my seat and walked quickly over to her, giving her a hug just as she started to cry.

"I'm so, so, so sorry." She continued to repeat over and over again.

I held her there for a long time, not sure what to say, and before I knew it, she was in my Dad's arms as he pointed to the kitchen counter where my toiletry bag and a pile of clothes sat.

I stood examining myself, in a tall mirror, in one of the bedrooms, in the cottage. My Dad had brought me over a pair of pale blue, cropped trouser, a white vest, and a pair of black sandals.

I pulled my favourite silver headband from the toiletry bag and gently slid it onto my head. Normally I would have spent ages adjusting my hair, so it would cover my birthmark, but for the first time, I pushed the headband back so my hair was off my face.

I smiled at my reflection. I don't think I'd ever felt this happy or self-assured before in my life.

I still had a million and one questions, but I'd been assured that Dr Hammersmith would explain everything later today. He was coming at 7pm. It was only 10:30am now, so I had the rest of the day to, hopefully, get to know Sean better.

After I neatly folded my pyjamas and placed them on one of the single beds, I checked and re-checked my appearance before heading out of the room.

I walked through the back door and out into the garden, which was surrounded by lots of trees. To me, it was more like a forest where a picturesque cottage sat in the middle with the sun shining straight down making everything glisten. My Dad was playing football with Sean, Paul, James, Kelly and Justin, whilst my Mum was pottering around in the flowerbeds.

I sat down on an old wooden bench underneath the kitchen window, with my head slightly tilted up towards the sun, whilst keeping one eye on the game.

Justin stood between two trees that were being used as make shift goal posts. The twins and Kelly were on one team, and my Dad and Sean on the other. I wasn't sure who was winning; I was just happy to watch.

They continued playing for another thirty minutes, when my Dad started complaining that he was too old and tired to keep up with the youngsters. Probably because he was only used to playing with my sister and me I knew I wasn't any good. A two year old had better ball control than me.

"I'm going to go home to take a shower and change my clothes." I heard Sean tell the others as my Dad sat next to me on the bench.

"You're getting old." I playfully teased my Dad, as Sean walked over to where we both sat.

"I'm a teenager at heart." My Dad smiled back at me, and then turned to face Sean, who was standing in front of us.

"I'm heading home for a bit." He pointed over his shoulder, as if he were pointing to a house that wasn't there. "You fancy coming?" he asked me as he held his hand out.

I looked at my Dad to see if it was okay.

"Sure, go ahead." He smiled as I reached up to take Sean's hand. "Just make sure you're back for dinner at 5pm."

We walked, hand in hand, towards the trees, at the edge of the clearing, where Justin still stood between the makeshift goal posts. I had no idea where Sean's house was or how far, it was just nice to take a walk alone with him.

All my life I'd dreamt that I would have a boyfriend. I still wasn't sure if Sean was my boyfriend or not. I hoped so. To be honest, I didn't feel I would ever get a boyfriend, but right now, whether or not he was, I felt I had hit the jackpot. I wasn't sure what would happen from now on, but I would be happy to spend my life in his arms, kissing his lips, and him stroking my cheek. I wish I was more spontaneous to make a move to kiss him. I felt nervous and swallowed hard as I remembered his warm lips pressing against mine. Without realising, my hand had reached up to touch my lips.

Quickly, I pulled my hand down as we reached a fence to a field that was full of baby's breath.

"Wow!" I gasped, "It's beautiful."

Without realising, Sean had released my hand and was standing with his back to me, leaning against the fence.

"Are we allowed to walk through here?" I asked nervously, as I started to climb the stile, he had used to get into the field. He waited on the other side, ready to catch me if I fell.

"I know the owner's very well." He smiled with a shrug, as I stepped past him, to start walking through the flowers with my arms stretched out on either side, my palms facing forward to catch the flowers as they brushed my fingertips.

I hadn't realised I was walking alone until I looked up, already a third of the way across the field. I looked around in panic searching for Sean. He was still leaning with his back against the fence watching me. I started to walk back towards him and stopped when I saw him start to hurry towards me. He wasn't smiling and I wasn't sure if I'd done something wrong. I looked at him confused and wanted to apologise for whatever I'd done. I felt sick with nerves, by the time he reached me, and he didn't stop moving.

He grabbed my face and started to kiss me fiercely. At first I just stood there, frozen. Then I started to kiss him back more urgently. One of my hands ran my fingers through his hair, as my other started to slowly run up and down his back.

To my embarrassment, I groaned as he pulled my head back by my hair and starting kissing my neck. My hand slipped to his bum and I heard and felt him laughing. His were lips vibrating on my neck, sending a shiver down my spine.

He laughed again, as he felt me tremble, then pulled away to look at me with a smile I was falling in love with. I chastised myself for thinking that last thought. It was too soon for me to be feeling this way. Wasn't it? I hardly knew him. He was surely going to break my heart. Hadn't I heard he used to have a different girl every week? What was this? Day one or day two? I decided yesterday didn't really count.

"Come on, let's go." He started pulling me through the field. I felt like I was floating more than walking.

We walked for a while. Not talking, as he led me to the end of the field and this time through a gate. We carried on walking, hand in hand, until we reached a row of houses.

"This is us." He pointed to the end house. "Not much, but its home and has been my whole life."

"It's lovely." I smiled, squeezing his hand, as he led me through the front door and into a spacious living room.

"My parents are at work. Just make yourself at home." He waved his hand around the room as he released my hand and gave me a quick kiss, "I'm going to take a quick shower. Won't be long." He said as he headed up the stairs.

I stood there for a few moments, looking at where he'd gone. Then I headed to the huge sofa and sat down, switching the TV on to the music channels.

I wasn't really paying attention to the TV as my eyes scanned the room, focusing on pictures on the far wall. I got up and walked slowly over to have a closer look.

They were all family pictures, spreading over decades. Lots of school pictures, pictures of Sean and Kelly holding various trophies, and a picture of... I think it was Kelly, ice skating, another of her riding a horse, and a picture of Sean in a football kit sitting on his team mate's shoulders, lifting a trophy.

In between them all was a giant picture of Sean and Kelly with their parents, one of those you get done in a professional studio.

My eyes fell on a picture, to the right of the large one. It was a picture of an old couple, maybe Sean's grandparents, but that wasn't what pulled me to the picture. I reached up to touch the face of the woman in the picture, at the same time touching my own cheek. I gasped and stepped back. The woman in the picture had a birthmark just like mine.

"My great grandparents." Sean spoke quietly, breaking my trance.

"But she's…" My voice trailed off, as I looked back at the picture.

"She was like you." He said, stepping closer.

He was wearing only a pair of jeans and was towel drying his hair, but he threw the towel on a chair, along with the top he was holding.

He stepped behind me, wrapping his arms around my waist.

"And my great grandfather," He pointed to the man in the picture, "was like me." I didn't understand. There had been someone else like me? Just like Sean? How was that possible?

Sensing my confusion he turned me to face him. His muscly chest was still damp and perfect in every way.

"I don't know much." He started to tell me as I moved my hands up to place them on his chest. "But I was told that my great grandfather could make it rain and manipulate water. I wasn't told any of this until I started to show the signs." He told me as an afterthought. I used my eyes to tell him to go on "It started half way through the last year of high school. Up to that point I thought I was happy." He pulled me onto the sofa, as he continued to talk. "I played every sport going and girls." He looked into my eyes, as he lay on his back, with me lying on top, with my chin resting on top of my hands, on his chest. "Well you know." He reached out to stroke my cheek, reassuringly. "But I started to sweat a lot, more than usual. I mean, I could run around a field and my clothes would be soaking. My parents even took me to the doctors, but they weren't sure why this was happening either, and it didn't even smell like sweat. "One day my parents took us to visit our grandparents, and it was there we found out what was wrong with me." He looked down at me, to see if I was bored yet, and I nodded at him to continue. "Well, I was in the garden with Kelly, when we heard something smash. We looked up to see Poppa shaking in shock, as he looked right at me. Apparently his Dad, my great grandfather was the exact same." He looked thoughtfully back to the picture, hanging on the wall. "He went on to tell me that eventually I would find my soul mate." He looked at me seriously, as he placed a finger on my left cheek "And that she would have the same mark as my great Nan." He gave me a quirky smile. He even looked slightly embarrassed.

"And that would be me, I suppose?" He laughed, and then nodded.

"To be honest, I thought it was a load of Mumbo jumbo." He laughed. "He kept telling me that as soon as I saw her everything would change and no matter how hard I tried, I wouldn't be able to keep away from her." He sighed then and rested his head back to look at the ceiling.

He didn't say anything for a while, as I ran my fingers around his chest, tracing the lines of water that were now drying up. Then he looked back at me, his face serious again.

"Then I saw you that day… murdering that orange." We both laughed. Then he stopped, turning serious once again, "You took my breath away."

I pondered this for a moment, continuing to trace the lines of water on his chest.

"Are you happy?" I suddenly asked thoughtfully, and before I knew it, he had pulled me further up his body, so our lips were nearly touching.

"I am now." He smiled, raising his head to kiss me.

We eventually came up for air, as he reached his hand to stroke my cheek.

"Fancy a drink?"

I nodded as he pulled me up and led me to the kitchen.

The kitchen was lovely, all oak cabinets with a breakfast bar and an oak table, which held a bowl of fruit in the centre. On one wall there were sliding doors that led into a conservatory and beyond that was the garden, which looked the size of a football pitch.

Whilst Sean went to pull out two glasses, I sat down at the breakfast bar.

Whilst I sat looking outside, Sean pulled out a carton of pure orange juice from the fridge.

"Orange okay?" I turned to look at him as he raised the carton.

"Yes, that fine!" I smiled, as I looked down at my hands, then back up to him, as he handed me my glass. "What do your parents do?" I asked as I moved the glass around in my hands before taking a drink.

"You know Peak Physique?" He asked as he took a mouthful of orange juice, and then turned to put the carton back in the fridge.

"That's the gym on Main Street, right?" He nodded as he leant on the other side of the breakfast bar, in front of me.

"My parents own that." He smiled at the shock in my face. "My Mum does all the accountancy side and deals with the memberships. My Dad does everything else, and me and Kelly help out after school and weekends." He finished his drink and went to put it in the dishwasher.

"Wow!" I was lost for words, I finished my drink. He shrugged and laughed as he took my glass. "Explains why you're so sporty." Which made him laugh more.

"Having a gym does have its advantages. I get free membership for a start." He went back to leaning in front of me. This time he reached out to hold my hands. Probably to stop me from fidgeting, as now I didn't have a glass to play with. "I'll give you a tour if you like?" I nodded at this offer.

Sure, visiting a gym wasn't something I would normally do, or ever have done, and if he'd asked

Kasey-Ray, she would have probably bitten his arm off in acceptance.

"My Dad would like to open another gym." He told me thoughtfully. "And he would like me to run one of them."

"What would you like to do?" I asked with interest.

He didn't answer me straight away. He moved round to where I sat and put his arms around me.

"I'm still undecided!" He leaned down to kiss me nearly distracting me from what we were talking about. "I'm studying sport's science. Something I applied for before I realised what I was." We both laughed at this. It did sound odd. "I still do like sports and keeping fit, but my heart isn't in it like it used to be." He looked past me, like his mind was wondering off to another world.

"Where is your heart?" My voice trembled, both at the thought of his heart and the fact I was having such an intimate conversation with this gorgeous boy. To me he was more of a man than a boy; he acted a lot older than all the 17 year old boys I'd seen.

He turned back and smiled at me for a while, and then he raised his hand and stroked my cheek.

"I don't know." He shook his head and looked away again. "All my life I wanted to follow in my Dad's footsteps. But when things changed, I was left feeling incomplete, like something was missing, like I had a bigger purpose in life. Does that sound wrong?" He turned to look at me for reassurance.

"No," I barely got out. He leaned down to kiss me again.

"Only one thing has become clearer though!" I looked at him puzzled, making him smile and kiss me. "I don't feel like there's something missing anymore." He laughed this time as I still looked at him in bewilderment, unsure by what he meant. "I found you!" He said each word clearly as he slowly started kissing me again, this time more passionately, and when he pulled away something caught his eye.

"Damn, we better get going." I followed his gaze and realised he was looking at the clock. "We'll take my car." He told me as I watched him longingly, as he pulled his t-shirt on. He laughed as he caught me looking, making me turn deep red as I looked away.

"Don't be embarrassed." He had stopped laughing as he pulled me off the stool and into his arms. "I like it when you look at me like that." My head was buried in his chest, not wanting to show my face. "It's nice to know that you feel the same way for me, as I feel for you."

I felt like I was dying here from embarrassment, then he comes out with a comment like that. I didn't think it was funny to joke like that. There was no way on earth that he could feel for me as I felt for him.

He bent his head down as he cupped my chin and slightly stepped away so I couldn't bury my face.

"Don't you believe me?" He sounded hurt. I slowly shook my head as I bit my lip, guilty for causing the pain in those beautiful eyes. "Then I'll just have to prove it to you." He kissed me again, pulling me close to his body. "Come on we better go." He said as he still had a tight hold of me, and he kept me there for a few more minutes, as he rested his head on the top of mine. Then he leant down and kissed me again, but this time when he pulled away he took my hand and walked me outside, grabbing his car keys on the way.

Chapter 9

We eventually got back to the cottage, just after 4pm. My Mum was busy in the kitchen, making dinner. Whatever it was, it smelt delicious. I stayed in the kitchen to help her, whilst Sean went into the other room.

As I was laying the table something dawned on me, "Kasey-Ray!" I said out loud, freezing where I stood.

My Mum looked over, understanding exactly what I meant.

"No, she doesn't know." She turned back to the pot. "And no, we have no idea if she has any gifts. We are hoping it may pass her by."

I nodded at this thoughtfully.

"When is she coming home? Is she coming here?"

"Your Dad's going to collect her just before Dr Hammersmith gets here, but he's taking her home first, to pack an overnight bag."

"How are we going to explain why we are here?" I finished laying the table and went to stand next to her.

"Not sure yet, but I'm sure she'll be more preoccupied with you and Sean." She laughed warmly, making me blush.

She carried on cooking, as I went into the other room. I walked up to the sofa, where Sean sat and leaned down to slide my hands down his chest.

"Hey you!" I whispered in his ear, as I kissed his cheek.

He smiled happily as he placed a hand on mine and the other he stretched up to slide his fingers through my hair and kiss me tenderly on the lips.

At 7pm sharp, there was a knock on the door. I was cuddled on the sofa with Sean, with one hand running though his hair. I paused as a tall man with long grey hair, tied into a pony-tail, wearing a grey suit and carrying a briefcase, stepped into the middle of the room and stared at me carefully. A slow smile spread across his face as he reached over to shake my free hand.

"You must be Erin!" It wasn't a question and he went to sit down in the arm chair, next to the fire, without taking his eyes off me. "I've waited a long time to finally meet you!" He saw my puzzled expression and raised his hands up, as he placed his briefcase at his feet. "All in good time."

He slowly looked at Sean, then back to me.

"It's wonderful that you two have finally found each other."

Sean moved uneasily in his seat and pulled me closer to him, protectively.

"It's okay, I'm not going to run any tests today." I looked at Sean and back to Dr Hammersmith, who eventually turned to look at me. "We will be running tests on you, like Sean said." *I hadn't heard Sean speak*, I thought, making Dr Hammersmith laugh.

He composed himself before continuing. "I'll need to test your strength. Your powers, so to speak."

I didn't like the sound of that, and feeling my unease, Sean reached up to gently stroke my left cheek.

Ignoring my unease, Dr Hammersmith continued to talk.

"Every century, one force dies and takes hold in another vessel, – body." His face was very serious as he leaned forward "The day that each of Sean's great grandparents died, you were both born, possessing their unique gifts."

Sean looked at me and I could tell he didn't realise this. He had told me that he had never gotten the chance to meet his great grandfather, as he had died when he was a baby, and his great grandmother had died a couple of years after. I could see the pain in his eyes as the velocity of this hit him and now we were being told that I was born on the day his great grandmother died. Bittersweet.

We looked at each other, and it was my turn to stroke his face. His eyes closed, as he placed my hand over his mouth to kiss it.

Dr Hammersmith was still talking. I'd heard him mention something about only children who were descendants of Galladale can possess the powers, and they all end up returning, which made me think of my parents.

"You will find it hard communicating with regular people from now on."

I laughed as soon as he said this. I'd always found it hard to communicate with regular people.

Then what he said next stopped me in my tracks.

"Especially now there are eight of you and in time there will be more."

"Eight?" I said out loud.

This time Dr Hammersmith was the one who looked puzzled.

"Yes Eight." He thought for a moment, as if he were counting. "You, Sean, Kate, John, Justin, Paul, James and Kelly. Yes that's definitely Eight."

I looked at Sean, who sheepishly looked away.

"Ahhhh" Dr Hammersmith said, with understanding. "No one has told you about the other four and their powers." He chuckled to himself. "Let me briefly explain." he said, looking at his watch, "Paul and James are magnets, north and south, so to speak. Kelly is..... Hmmm, how can I say this? She is an EMP. Electrical magnetic pulse, and she is the glue that holds Paul and James together. Very special and powerful force them three." He smiled to himself, as he thought about them. "Justin is a trainer, and well you know what your parents are."

"Trainer?" I wanted to know what a trainer was, but Dr Hammersmith was ignoring me, and rooting in his briefcase.

"I would like to see you both next week." He told us and he pulled something from his briefcase. "Here is your I.D card, to get in." He handed me a plastic card with my name on. Then he closed his briefcase and stood up. "I look forward to seeing you both." Then he was gone.

I sat there for a few minutes, staring after him, as I tried to get my head around what had just been said. I was about to turn and ask Sean when Kasey-Ray came bounding in.

"Well ain't this a quaint place!" She grimaced, as she fell back on the sofa, next to me.

I didn't speak, but watched her carefully as she lay there with her eyes closed.

Slowly, she opened one eye to look at me, then the other as she spotted Sean's arm around me, and slowly she sat up to look at Sean.

"Hey I know you, don't I?" She asked as she looked from his face, to mine, and then back to his, "Jacko isn't it?"

Sean smiled and nodded, "That's right!"

"Sean, his name is Sean." I corrected her.

"Touchy." She laughed and raised her eyebrows at Sean. "So what are you doing here?"

Anger slowly started to build up inside me. Sensing this, Sean looked at Kasey-Ray and squeezed my hand.

"Cos I'm in love with your sister!" I froze. *We were still on day one. How could he love me?* Of course I felt like I was in love with him too. I'd never felt like this about anyone before.

I hadn't realised they were both watching me. Had they asked me something?

"Well?" Kasey-Ray pressed.

"Sorry what?" I shook my head and looked at my sister. She sighed and shook her head.

"Do you love him?" She pointed from me to Sean. "Duh!"

I looked at Sean, who was staring intently into my eyes, like I had his heart in my hands and I could squash it at any time.

I nodded and touched his face, "Yes!"

The relief in his face was unreal. I am sure that, one day, I would get my head around how this beautiful person could love me so much. But I doubted that.

I was still smiling when he kissed me. When he pulled away he sat there staring into my eyes, as Kasey-Ray started talking about her date.

Apparently, everything had gone well, but she wasn't sure if she was into him as much as she thought.

"Anyway, where are the bedrooms in this place?"

That night I shared a double bed with Kasey-Ray, whilst Sean stayed in one of the single beds, on the side of the room where I was.

After Kasey-Ray had talked my ears off, I rolled over to face Sean, as he lay there watching me.

He reached over to hold one of my hands, and we stayed like that until we fell asleep.

The sun was shining brightly, pulling me from my sleep. I was lying on my back, staring at the ceiling when someone's arms smacked across my face.

"Ow," I cried in pain, pushing my sister's arm back, which didn't even wake her. I sat up and looked around the room and at the empty bed, where Sean had slept.

I walked sleepily out of the room, and after a detour to the bathroom, I trudged to the kitchen, where I had heard voices coming from.

Sean, who was sat eating a bowl of cereal, looked up when I got to the doorway. He smiled and reached out to pull me onto his lap, and after a quick kiss he continued eating, even offering me a bite.

"We're going to head home after lunch." My Mum said, without looking up from her own breakfast.

"Okay!" I nodded, as I slid off Sean's lap to go make myself some toast.

After lunch, Kasey-Ray, my Mum and I climbed into my parent's car, as my Dad went to make sure that everything was locked up.

Sean was at my window, stroking my face.

"I'll pop over after dinner, if that's okay?" He leaned over and kissed me. I just nodded.

We hadn't been apart for the whole two days and I felt like my heart was being pulled out. I didn't want to feel needy or clingy. I just wanted him to be there when I got home.

He stood staring after me as we pulled away.

***

It was only a few hours, but time seemed to drag. I stayed in my room the whole time, sitting on my window seat, staring out of the window waiting for him. I didn't eat my dinner, even when my Dad brought it up to me. He had told me that he was keeping Kasey-Ray out of my room, in case I set her on fire. This made me laugh.

At 5:58pm, I saw his orange Ford Focus ST, pull into the drive and I almost flew down the stairs and into his arms. I smothered him in kisses, making him laugh as he kissed me back, whilst keeping a tight grip of me.

"You want to go grab something to eat?" He pointed at his car. I wasn't sure if my stomach rumbling had given me away or not.

"Uh-huh" I happily said, as he carried me round to the passenger seat. I wasn't sure where he was taking me, but as long as I was with him, I didn't care.

I didn't have to wait long to find out, as we pulled into the car park at his family's gym.

"I thought we were going for something to eat?" I asked puzzled.

"We are." He laughed as he climbed out the car and came round to hold my hand. "I thought we could eat here." I raised one eyebrow at him. *Was there something he wasn't telling me?* "We have a nice little cafe here you know!" He smiled as he led the way. *Ahhh well that would explain it.* "Also, I thought you could meet my parents." I stopped dead, panic spreading across my face. "They don't bite." He tried to assure me, as he stepped in front of me to stroke my face.

"I couldn't find the right words to say, but before I could he was already talking.

"They know everything, and they've wanted to meet you for a long time."

"But..."

"But nothing." He ran his fingers across my lips. I was so scared. *What if they didn't like me? What if they took one look at my birthmark and were repulsed by me and wondered what their son saw in someone like me?* I could feel the panic rising even more at all the questions that were spinning around my head.

"Come on, for me please?" He leaned down to kiss me softly. "I promise everything will be fine." How could I refuse him? I sighed as I pulled away, and looked at him seriously.

"I am only doing this cos you asked me to!" A huge smile crossed his face as he took my hand again. Taking a deep breath I let him guide me into the building.

"Hi Samantha." He smiled and nodded at the girl at the reception desk.

"Hi Sean." She giggled. Even the way she said it oozed, 'I want you', out of every pore, making me want to slap her. I protectively moved to grab his hand, I was already holding, with my other.

"My Mum in the office?" He asked, not stopping as he walked past.

"Yes, she sure is." I couldn't blame her for acting that way, I probably would be too, or probably was and didn't realise it, but didn't she see me holding his hand? Probably not I was just some plain Jane who she probably thought was lost and he was helping me out.

She was attractive. Her brown hair was tied in a neat ponytail, her make up perfectly applied, and her body did look amazing, even in the tracksuit she was wearing.

She'd probably thrown herself at him many times and he had probably even dated her. I shivered at this thought, trying to shake it out of my head

"You okay?" He looked at me, trying to study my face.

"Yeah fine!" I forced a smile. I didn't want to tell him that I was just picturing him with that Samantha girl.

We walked the short way down a corridor, plastered with all sorts of posters on fitness, and then he knocked on the final door, next to the staff room.

"Come in." I heard the polite voice of a woman call, from the other side.

Slowly Sean opened the door, as I hid behind him.

"Hi Mum." He said as he walked through the door, almost dragging me in behind him.

"Hi son." I heard her reply. I still hadn't plucked up the courage to look round.

"I want you to meet someone!" He turned to move me to his side.

The woman sitting behind a table, full of a pile of paperwork looked past Sean and right at me.

"You must be Erin." She smiled warmly as she got up from her seat and walked round to give me a hug. "I've heard so much about you!" I nervously looked from her to Sean then back again.

"Hi." I smiled sheepishly, my throat beginning to dry up, "All good I hope." I laughed nervously.

"Very much so." She laughed, "I was beginning to think he'd made you up." She stepped away then to sit on the edge of her desk. I would say she was in her late thirty's and at least 5'10" or that could have been her heels. She had short brown hair and red glasses, which emphasised her beautiful face. I could definitely see where Sean got his good looks from.

Sean moved back to my side and put his arm around my waist, pulling me protectively towards him.

"So what brings you two here?" She was still smiling as she took her glasses off and placed them on top of her head.

"I thought Erin may like to try some of Wendy's cooking. Is she still working?" I had no idea who Wendy was.

"Yes, she doesn't finish 'til 8pm."

"Okay, we are going to go eat." Sean started leading me out the door.

"Don't be a stranger Erin; pop in anytime. The door is always open!" She called after us.

"What's your Mum's name?"

"Sorry." He laughed, as he put his hand to his head, "Ruth and my Dad is called Brian. You will get to meet him after we've eaten." I nodded and smiled at him.

"She's nice," and I meant it. His Mum was really warm and friendly, and looked genuinely happy to see me. I also liked the fact that he had apparently been talking about me and for a long time as well.

"And she seemed to like you too." He pulled me close to kiss the top of my head, as we reached a set of double doors that read 'Wendy's Cafe' above.

"Who's Wendy?"

"She's my adoptive Gran." He smiled fondly as he mentioned her. "And she is the best cook I've ever met."

"Sean!" I heard a stout, robust lady call as we stepped through the double doors of the blue and green cafe. I'd never actually known there was a cafe in the gym. I would have to tell my parents. "To what do I owe the pleasure?" She asked as she released him from her embrace, and turned to look at me "Oooooh, this must be Erin?" She looked back to Sean, with a look saying she was hoped she was right.

"It sure is!" He said as he took my hand.

"Well, ain't you the cutest wee thing!" She said as she quickly embraced me in a tight squeeze. *Well*

I've never been called that before. I laughed to myself.

"I thought I would let Erin try some of your wonderful cooking." He smiled lovingly at her.

"Well, you are in luck." She turned to walk away. "I'll just pulled some lasagne out of the oven. Be back in a mo." Then she disappeared through another set of double doors, which I assumed was the kitchen.

"You okay?" He asked me again, as he led me to a table in the middle.

"Yeah, I'm fine." I nodded as I looked around. There were only two other people in here. They looked like they had just been for a workout and were happily digging into a salad.

"Sure?" he squeezed my hands gently, making me bring my eyes back to the table.

"Yes." I smiled as I looked into his eyes. I wasn't used to all this friendly attention. I was starting to feel slightly intimidated.

"I love you, you know." He picked up my hands and leant down to kiss them. It was only the second time he'd said that, and I was still unsure if I fully believed it. I couldn't get my head around it.

"I love you too." My heart catching in my throat, my face was turning red. This was going to take some getting used to. It may be easy for me to love him as deeply as I did, but saying it was hard, mainly because I was sure that I would end up with a broken heart.

"Here you go!" Wendy was back with 2 plates of steaming lasagne and salad. "Tuck in." She smiled at me warmly. She stood there watching me and I realised she wasn't going to leave the table until I had actually tried it.

Nervously I picked up a fork and gently stabbed it into the lasagne, it came away so easily, apart from the stringy cheese that didn't seem to want to separate from my fork or plate. Using my fingers I gently separated it, blushing as I realised her eyes were still on me.

Carefully placing my hand under the fork, I slipped it into my mouth. I wasn't sure what I was expecting but this certainly wasn't it.

"Wow." I said with a mouth full of lasagne. Sean laughed as he gave me a triumphant smile. It was like it was melting in my mouth. I don't think I'd ever tasted lasagne this good.

"What are you up to this evening?" Wendy was still standing there. I was kind of oblivious now as I ate her delicious food.

"We are going to the DVD shop after this. Erin's family have a DVD night every Friday." I stopped eating to look at him. I had actually forgotten it was Friday.

"That's nice." she told him. "Well, I'll leave you to it." She started to turn away, but looked back at me. "Nice meeting you, Erin! Don't be a stranger, okay?" I nodded, knowing full well that I would probably want to move in here with food like this.

"You too." I smiled as I took another forkful. "I can't believe it's Friday already." I looked back at Sean, who was already half way through his food.

"I hadn't forgotten. I was going to come with you all, but your Dad texted me to say you hadn't eaten, so I thought I could bring you here first and meet the rest of my family and meet your family at the DVD shop later."

I groaned at the fact my Dad had told on me, but I was slightly happy, as I wouldn't be sitting here right now eating this heavenly food.

"She really is a great cook." I said as I pushed my empty plate away.

"I told you." Sean laughed. He'd already finished, and had sat patiently waiting for me to finish. I probably could have eaten quicker but I was afraid that if I rushed, the food would probably end up all over my clothes.

"Are we heading to the DVD shop now?"

"Just got to take you to meet my Dad." he smiled nervously. A fresh wave of nerves swept over me again, almost making me feel sick, and I did not want to bring up the food I'd just eaten, I didn't think Wendy would feel like such a good cook if I did that.

"You okay?" He reached over to hold my hand. I smiled weakly and nodded. "Come on let's get this over with." He stood up, still holding my hand, pulling me to my feet. "See ya later Wendy!" Sean called as he waved.

"Bye." She waved as I waved back, as I cuddled into Sean's side.

I half walked and was half pulled out of the cafe and along the corridor. When we reached reception Samantha was talking on the phone and when she spotted Sean she seemed to smile and flutter her eyelashes as she gave him a small wave. *Hello I'm here too ya know*.

Sean was oblivious as he peered through the circular windows, and then knocked on the glass. He took a step back, pulling me with him, as a smallish, muscular man with thinning hair appeared.

He seemed to be distracted as he kept looking back through the doors.

"Everything okay?" He hadn't even looked at me yet.

"Everything's fine, I just wanted to quickly introduce you to Erin." He turned then and almost gasped as he looked at me, but not in repulsion. More from amazement as it seemed to pull him from whatever was distracting him.

"Erin." He barely got out. His eyes kept looking to my birthmark, making me feel self conscious.

"Dad!" Sean firmly and sharply said his name.

"What?" He looked to Sean then back to me, obviously seeing me looking uncomfortable. "Oh, sorry" He quickly apologised, looking back to Sean then to me again, as he held out his hand. "I am really sorry, it's just..." His voice trailed off as he looked back to Sean, questioning him with his eyes, then back to me. "You look like my Gran." He blushed then as the realisation dawned on me. "I didn't think I looked like the woman in the picture, but I could understand, with me sharing the same type of birthmark on the same side of my face. It must be hard for him seeing me.

"Dad." Sean spoke again.

"Yeah, I know, I'm sorry, I just didn't fully realise." He nodded without taking his eyes off me. "It was really nice to meet you." He reached his hand to stroke my arm. "I would love to see you again when I'm not as busy." He smiled apologetically.

Before anything else was said he nodded and disappeared through the same doors he'd come from.

"Wow," I gulped, when he'd gone.

"I'm so sorry." Sean apologised as he led me through the main doors. "I did tell him. I think." he said mainly to himself.

"Don't worry about it." I didn't want him to beat himself up over it. His Dad hadn't been repulsed by me, even if that's what I had thought at the beginning.

"Don't say that." He stopped in front of his car. "That was so bloody rude." He was angry now as he leaned on the bonnet of his car. I stepped in front of him and watched him rub his temples, in an attempt to calm down. "Right now I want to go and drag him out here." He stood up and pointed towards the gym.

"Sean?" He stopped to look at me. For a second, I thought he was going to shout at me, then his face calmed as he reached out to stroke my left cheek.

"Sorry." He pulled me into his arms. "I never want you to get hurt or feel pain." I looked up to his agonised face.

"Sean?" It was my turn to stroke his face. "It's okay." I put my finger to his lips as he tried to speak. "Don't! Your Dad meant no harm. Don't give him a hard time, cos he is probably feeling guilty." I released my finger and stroked his cheek. He sighed then and leaned down to lightly kiss me.

"Come on, we best go meet up with your family before I get grief." He finally smiled as he released me and made his way to the driver's seat.

Chapter 10

By the time we walked into the DVD shop my Dad was already in the queue, ready to take the DVD's home.

"Sorry." Sean told him.

"It's fine, you'll just have to make do with our selection." My Dad laughed.

"I'm sure they'll be fine."

"Are you still going for pizza?" I asked. I wasn't really hungry but it kind of was our family tradition.

"We are, but haven't you just eaten?" He looked critically at Sean.

"Yeah we have. I was just going to say that if you are then me and Sean will just head back to the house, if that's okay?"

"Oh yeah, sure, that's fine." My Dad reached into his trouser pocket and pulled out his keys. "Here."

He said as he unfastened the front door key from his car keys. "We shouldn't be too long."

Taking the key from his hand, I waved at my family. By now, my Mum and sister had come to join my Dad, laden down with goodies. I had no idea why they bought them when they were getting a pizza, plus we had a fully stocked junk food cupboard.

"You didn't want a pizza did you?" I asked, feeling guilty, as I climbed into the passenger seat of Sean's car.

"No, no, I'm good." He squeezed my leg in reassurance, and then reversed out of the car park.

"Hey, I just realised something!"

"What's that?" He asked with his eyes still on the road.

"You never got a text message." He briefly looked at me with a puzzled expression. "What I mean is..." *Hmmm how do I word this?* "Every Friday night I've seen you, you get a message and leave."

"Ahhhh..." He laughed as he realised what I was getting at. I was still confused as something else dawned on me.

"Hang on a minute." I raised a finger as he pulled up outside my house and went to climb out. "Did you ever get a DVD?"

"No." He laughed again, even more so when he saw how confused I was. "I'll explain inside." He was already out of the car before I could stop him.

Quickly I followed, pulling out the front door key. The sooner we got inside the sooner I would understand, I hoped.

"Tell me." I said as soon as I had hung up the key and shut the door behind me.

"Okay." He walked to the sofa, pulling me behind him. "Sit." I quickly obeyed, sitting cross legged on the sofa next to him. "I knew you and your family rented movies every week, and it was my only way to be near you without Jessica finding out." He paused for a moment as I waited for the punch line. "The messages were from Kelly or the twins. They all went bowling every Friday night with Justin and Jessica." I was still confused. "They have to go past there and my car sticks out like a sore thumb." He laughed, and I had to admit it was a bit bright, and you could spot it a mile off.

"You were stalking me?" I asked, both shocked and flattered, making him laugh more.

"Kind of..." He reached up to my face. "As soon as I saw you on the field, I knew I had to find out more about you."

"How? Why?" I didn't know what else to say. I actually felt like crying. Not from being upset, but by the fact he went to such efforts.

"It was quite easy when I found out who your parents were." He smiled with a shrug, and before he could continue Kasey-Ray thundered in, removing everything off the table.

"You okay Krazy-Rabies?" Using the nickname we often called her, whilst wondering what the rush was.

"Dad got a huge pizza. 16 inches I think." She stood up to examine the table. "I hope it's big enough." She laughed to herself, completely making me forget my conversation with Sean as my Dad struggled to get the pizza box through the door.

"Got a bigger one in case you two change your mind and decide you're hungry." He laughed as he balanced the box like he was auditioning for an act in a circus. All he would need to do was trip, send the pizza flying and he would get the part of a clown.

Eventually we all sat down to watch a movie. By the time the second one was over, Sean got up from next to me and stretched with a yawn.

"I'm going to head home." He looked at the others before me, and then reached out to take my hand, as he led me to the front door.

Stepping outside, he pulled me into his arms and leaned down to kiss me.

"Tomorrow, I'm taking you somewhere." He released my lips and stroked my face.

"Where?" I breathlessly asked.

"You'll see." He winked and kissed me again. "I'll pick you up at ten." He kissed me again, then pulled out his keys as he headed towards his car. "I'll text you later." He waved as he climbed in the car.

I wished he never had to leave. The night would seem so long without him.

I stood there waving until I couldn't see his car any more. Eventually I turned to rejoin my family.

***

At 9:45am, I received a text from Sean to say he was on his way. After a quick check in the mirror, I quickly ran down the stairs.

"Bye." I shouted to anyone who was listening as I ran out the front door, slamming it shut behind me.

I didn't have to wait long, as I saw his car pull into my street.

"Hi." I happily sang as I climbed into the passenger seat.

"Hey you." He leaned over to kiss me. "How you feeling?" He turned back to the road as he pulled away.

"Great." I smiled, and I meant it. Every time I saw him I felt blissfully happy. "So where are we going?" I looked around, hoping for a clue.

"You'll have to wait till we get there." He winked.

We hadn't been driving for long when we turned into a small car park, surrounded by lots of trees.

Before we'd even parked the car just stopped. Sean tried to start it again, but nothing happened. He hit his steering wheel with mild frustration.

"Where the heck are you?" He said more to himself as he looked through the window, towards the trees. I had no idea who he was talking about and before I could ask, the car started to move forward, making me scream.

"It's okay." Sean tried to reassure me. "Look!" He pointed out of the windscreen as the car stopped, and there I saw Kelly, Paul and James laughing as I slowly started to understand, but not completely. "Not frigging funny!" Sean shouted as he jumped out of the car.

I stayed there, glued to my seat. I was feeling pretty shaken up, still unsure what had happened exactly. I could hear Sean still shouting, but I had tuned out what was being said. I was still trying to get my head around what had just happened. I hadn't even noticed my door opening as Sean knelt down.

"Erin?" He soothed as he tried to remove my hands from where they firmly gripped the seat. "Erin?" I slowly looked towards him as I realised he was there talking to me. I smiled at him as he managed to release my hands and reach over to undo my seat belt.

Quietly he helped me out of the car, shutting the door behind me.

"Erin, I'm so sorry." Kelly stepped in front of me and reached out to give me a hug. "I forget you're not used to us all and our powers."

"You did that?" I pointed towards the car

"And Paul." She nodded with a nervous laugh.

"Cool trick." I smiled, making everyone laugh.

"You okay?" Sean whispered as Kelly went back to high five the twins.

"Yeah." I sighed with a smile as I turned to look at him, "I'm fine, just a bit shocked."

"Sorry, I should have explained in more detail what they can do." He walked to open the boot of the car and pulled out a bag and a blanket. "Kelly's just learnt to focus her powers on one object. Before she would stop everything electrical for miles." He laughed at this thought as he locked the car. "She can still do that, but it causes problems with most people not knowing about us."

We started to walk slowly, following Kelly, Paul and James.

"Who pulled the car?" I was intrigued by it all. All I could do was produce flames, but to turn off everything electrical was cool, in my opinion.

"That would be Paul." He started to point to the twins, like he was trying to figure out who was who. "I still can't tell them apart." He laughed. "And James," By this time he'd given up trying to decide who was who. "He pushes things away." I nodded with understanding. Things were just getting more and more interesting. I'd never thought my summer holidays would ever be like this. It was like a real adventure, plus I got to spend it with the best looking person in the world.

We'd finally stopped as Sean put the bag down and started laying the blanket on the floor. I'd already noticed there was another blanket next to this and a pile of sporting items, as Kelly picked up a football and volleyed it.

Watching where the ball had gone, I stood there, slowly turning around, taking in my surroundings. We were in a huge open field, with a large lake. I could see for miles around, even if it was mainly fields and hills. It was all so breathtaking.

"Wow, it's beautiful." I smiled as I finally turned to look at Sean, who was now sitting on the blanket. I sat down next to him, half facing the lake whilst watching Kelly and the twins playing football.

"Nice isn't it?"

"It sure is." I turned to look at him. "What's that in the lake?" I pointed towards a large, what looked like a rock, protruding in the centre. Sean followed to where I was pointing.

"That's the reason we are like this." I looked back at him to check he was actually looking at what I was pointing at.

"You like talking in riddles, don't you?" I wasn't slightly annoyed that he wasn't giving me a straight answer.

"It's the reason I brought you here. So I can explain." He defended as he emphasised on the word can.

"I'm listening." I said when he paused.

"I'm not sure what it is exactly, no one does. But several hundreds of years ago it wasn't there, and then something fell from the sky." He waved his hand up and down as he explained. "The people of Galladale came to see what it was. Now bear in mind there weren't as many people living here back then and they didn't know what it was, some even swam out to get a closer look." He paused again as he looked towards the lake. "If you look closely it looks like a giant lump of coal." I squinted my eyes to look at it.

"Oh yeah."

"People said they could hear a humming coming from it. One person leant her face closer to try and listen, but she got too close and it must have been hot, because she ended up burning her face." He paused to reach up to my birthmark. "Her left cheek." I almost flinched at this thought. "There was a man close to her and he was able to cool her cheek, but she was scarred for life." It all sounded a bit farfetched, but I knew it must be true.

"Anyway." He continued as he lay down on his back. "Everyone started to get sick. They didn't realise at the time, that they were changing." He pulled me down next to him. "From that day, Galladale was never the same. At first people worried about the next generation, whether their powers would be passed on. After only a few decades this had only happened once or twice, so they thought it was something that would die out. They didn't know that whenever someone died the child born on that day would inherit their powers, even if not blood related."

"Wowsers!" I looked up to the sky, trying to take it all in "Does that mean everyone who lives here knows?"

"No." Which made me roll onto my side to look at him. "Some people refused to talk about it and were relieved when it skipped so many generations, so there was no need."

"But there will be some who have heard the stories."

"Yeah, but we all thought they were myths." He laughed "Me included."

"So how do you know all this?"

"My Poppa had heard all the stories, as his parents were like you and I. So of course he knew it was the truth. My Dad had been told the stories but as he grew up he just thought of them as bedtime stories." He laughed as he sat up to pick up the football that had just landed at our feet and threw it back towards the shouting trio.

"I wonder why my parents didn't tell me?" I said mainly to myself.

"Like I said, they hoped it would miss a generation."

Then I remembered them telling me the same thing.

"You know what is funny?" Sean interrupted my thoughts. "My Mum had no ties to Galladale, so my Poppa isn't sure if it's a first that someone from outside gave birth to not one, but two of us."

"I hadn't actually thought about that.

"Sean?" I heard Kelly shout as she was waving him towards her.

"Not now."

"Who discovered theirs first?" I nodded from him to Kelly.

"Good question. My Poppa noticed mine first, then a few weeks later spotted Kelly's, after she was throwing a paddy over me being distant." He laughed as he looked at his sister "But she says she had been able to do things like that for a long time." He pointed through the trees, where we had walked through, to the car park. "Which is plausible, cos she has been able to control her powers quicker than me."

"What about the twins?"

"Apparently they've been like that since birth and they used to fight all the time."

"Then they met Kelly." I said with understanding

"Well, not really. They were in her year at school. Not that she noticed them." He laughed. "They used to follow her around and fight over her." He laughed shaking his head like he didn't understand their fascination with his big sister. "But when she figured out her powers, she noticed them."

"Is she with either of them?" I was intrigued, but this made Sean laugh. "What's so funny?"

"She's with both of them." I stared at him with a disgusted expression, making him laugh even more.

"And they know?" He nodded, trying to control his laughter. "And they don't mind?"

"Not at all! It actually made them get on better. Apparently before them there was only one person who possessed both their powers and when he died, Paul and James were born, so the powers were split." I was understanding that, but she was with both of them. I shook my head in utter disbelief. "You'll get used to it, and you will see there's nothing gross about it."

"I don't know about that. I couldn't share with anyone." He smiled at this and leaned over to kiss me.

"And I wouldn't share you with anyone either."

We lay there for a while, in each other's arms, until Sean sat up.

"Anyway." He pulled the bag he'd taken out of the car onto his lap. "I brought some food, so we can have a picnic. You hungry?"

"Starving."

Chapter 11

The next day, I woke up feeling refreshed and happy. It didn't take me long to realise why as my mobile phone buzzed with a text message.

'Morning baby, I hope you slept well. See you later.
I love you x'

He never actually called me baby out loud, and every time I read that one word, I felt all warm and fuzzy. He always finished by telling me he loved me. That was still going to take some getting used to. Only my family ever told me they loved me. I still felt awkward saying it. I expected him to laugh in my face and tell me it was all some big joke. Just the mere thought of that made me feel like my heart was being squeezed hard.

Before the feeling got the better of me, I quickly hit reply and typed out a message.

'Morning. Have fun at practice. I love you too. See you later x'

I still felt awkward giving him a pet name, and thought if I put I loved him, somewhere in the middle, then that would be okay.

This morning Sean was off to football practice and was going to come over afterwards.

Slowly, I climbed out of bed and made my way to the bathroom. After I'd finished washing my face, I stopped to look at my reflection. It hadn't even been a week and you could see a significant difference in my birthmark. It looked smoother, somehow smaller.

Sean had told me that when I controlled the fire in me, then my birthmark would fade. Only one thing confused me. If Sean's great grandmother had had the same powers, then why did she still have the birthmark in the picture I'd seen? It was something I would need to ask him.

I felt happiness at the thought of my birthmark disappearing, but if it was a case where it would come back, I wasn't sure if I could handle that.

Walking back to my bedroom, I ran into Kasey-Ray on the landing as she headed towards her room.

"You been for a run?"

My sister was sporty, but she rarely went running. It was mainly on the treadmill at the gym, in our home town. I don't think she'd actually been to Sean's family gym yet.

"Yeah." She breathed heavily. "There's something about this place that feels so exhilarating." I laughed at the use of her big word. "You should try it." She told me seriously.

"I don't think so." I scoffed. I was allergic to any type of exercise.

"I'm sure you would if Sean asked you." She winked as she followed me into my room.

"Definitely not." I shook my head. The idea of getting all hot, sweaty and out of breath was not my idea of exhilaration.

"You two are such opposites." This hurt! I knew this already and often doubted why he was interested in me. "That's not a bad thing." She quickly added. "They say opposites attract." She walked over to sit on my window seat, whilst watching my reaction. I said nothing as I went to look for something to wear.

She continued to sit there, turning to look out of the window.

"I will say one thing though." I raised an eyebrow waiting for another kick in the stomach. I just had to tell myself not to get angry. I wasn't ready to tell her about these powers, or whatever they were, especially when I didn't understand them myself.

"He looks at you like you are..." She paused as she tried to find the right words, "like you are the most important and most beautiful person alive. He looks at you with complete adoration." She sighed and at first I took it as though she was disgusted or she couldn't understand why. "I'm jealous." She finally said, stopping my anger dead in its tracks.

"Why?" I turned to her in confusion. I was always jealous of my sister; she could have any boy she wanted. Everyone wanted to be her friend.

"You're so happy and have someone who loves you for you." She sighed and turned back to look out of the window. "I've never had that. I wish I could find someone who looked at me like Jacko… I mean Sean, looks at you."

"What are you talking about?" I'd seen the way all the boys looked at her, like they wished she was theirs. "Most lads would give their right arms to be with you."

"It's not the same."

"What about Matt?" I'd seen the way he looked at her and to me it seemed like there was only one person for him.

"Ah, Matt." She grimaced at the mere mention of his name. "I was more of a trophy." She rolled her eyes. "When people were around he was very attentive. Opening doors, arms around me, kissing me, but as soon as we were alone it was like a whole different person. He went quiet, gave me one word answers and the only time he got excited was when the subject was about him." She laughed, but not a full hearty laugh that normally reached her eyes.

She shrugged and stood up. I didn't really know what to say. I'd always seen Kasey-Ray as my happy little sister, who could have anything she wanted.

"You look really happy and I am happy that you are. I am also happy that someone else has seen how beautiful you are, rather than judging you on your birthmark." She smiled as she started towards my bedroom door, leaving me standing there, open-mouthed. "You know I've always wished I was like you."

"Me?" This comment floored me.

"You've always been happy with who you are on the inside." She nodded.

"But you're beautiful and everyone wants to be like you." I scoffed.

"All superficial." She waved as though brushing my comment away. "You know who you can and can't trust." She pointed out. This was true, in a way. I could trust my family, as I'd never gotten close enough to trust anyone else, and I was now slowly trusting Sean, even though most of the time I felt like I kept a ten foot wall up around me.

"What about Claire?" She seemed to have a good friendship with her, even though I didn't like her.

"Hmmm..." She leant on my door frame. "Before we moved here, Claire wasn't popular. Don't get me wrong, she hasn't done anything wrong, but sometimes I feel that if I wasn't popular then she wouldn't give me the time of day."

To be honest, I actually agreed with Kasey-Ray, but it wasn't something I would have voiced.

"Anyway." She sighed, "I'm off to get a shower." She waved, leaving me reeling from our conversation.

After a couple of minutes I shook my head then continued to get dressed. I pulled on a knee length beige skirt with a white vest and slipped on a pair of corked sandals.

Standing in front of the mirror, I played about with my hair, trying to decide how to wear it. I still wasn't brave enough to have it all tied back, but I decided to compromise and put the top part of my hair back off my face into a clasp at the back of my head.

Smiling at my reflection, I turned to head downstairs to find something for breakfast.

The house seemed empty, apart from the sound of music blasting from Kasey-Ray's bedroom. I walked into the kitchen and decided to settle for a bowl of cereal. Half way through eating, my Mum appeared from outside.

"Hi." I Mumbled with a mouthful of cereal.

"Hey." My Mum cheerily sang as she put the empty washing basket in the cupboard. "Where you off to today?" She asked as she busied in the already pristine kitchen.

"No idea." I shrugged.

"You are seeing Sean today aren't you?" She looked up from the worktop she was wiping for the third time.

My Mum was a bit of a clean freak. My Dad always joked that she had OCD. The house was always immaculate and if someone so much as moved a grain of salt, she would know, even if we thought it was back in the exact same place.

It was understandable that she cleaned people's homes for a living. She often told us that why would she work in an office when she could do a job she really enjoyed.

"Uh-huh. He's playing football this morning." I finished my cereal and walked over and put my empty bowl in the sink.

"Well, whilst you are waiting, can you go make sure your bedroom is tidy please." I nodded and did as I was told, even though I knew that she would be in my room later cleaning it herself.

Luckily I only had my bed to make, which took less than a minute to sort.

When I'd finished I did another check in the mirror, just in case one thing was out of place, and then I headed downstairs, bumping into Kasey-Ray on the way.

"What are you up to today?" I asked her as we walked side by side down the stairs.

"I haven't decided yet, I may give Claire a call." She shrugged. "You?"

"Not sure yet. Sean said he was coming for me after football. I don't know if he's going home first or not."

I didn't even think to ask him what we were doing. I was just happy that he wanted to spend time with me.

We were about to sit down on the sofa when we noticed our Mum had pulled the hoover out.

"Why don't you girls go outside and enjoy the sunshine." She told us with a smile, which translated as, 'Get out of my way, I'm cleaning.' I almost laughed at this translation as I followed my sister out the back.

We lay down on the grass, not bothering with blankets.

"What do you want in a boyfriend?" I asked my sister thoughtfully, as I started picking daisies to make a daisy chain.

"Mmmm..." She propped her head up on one arm to look at me. "Obviously he has to be good looking." She laughed. "Errrr, he needs to want to be with me for me, not how I look." I laughed this time, as it was similar to what I looked for but we were on different levels. Whereas she wanted people to see past her good looks, I wanted people to see past my birthmark.

"He has to make me laugh, and be the same with me no matter if we are alone or there's a million people around us." She sighed. "It feels like I'm asking for a miracle at times."

"I don't think you are." I said, as I leaned forward to put the daisy chain around her neck. "I never thought it would happen to me, and I still feel like I'm dreaming."

Just then I squealed in pain as Kasey-Ray punched me.

"What was that for?"

"If you were dreaming then you'd have woken up by now." She smiled with a laugh. "It's all real. Sean is real. The way he wants to be with you is real."

"But I'm scared!" I almost cried, making my sister quickly sit up and look at me, as she reached over to touch my arm.

"Why? What are you scared of?"

"It seems too good to be true. Why would he want me? He could have anyone he wanted. I keep expecting him to say he's with me for a bet." Tears were now starting to fall from my eyes, as Kasey-Ray pulled me into her arms.

"You're beautiful."

"And you're biased. I'm a hideous freak!"

"Hey!" Kasey-Ray held me firmly at arm's length. "Don't you dare say that. Yes, you have a birthmark on your face, but so what? You are beautiful both inside and out." She lightly shook me as I tried to control my tears. "Look, if I thought for one second that Sean was doing this for a stupid bet, then I wouldn't let him anywhere near you." She spat. "You may be my big sister, but I feel it's my job to look out for you and if anyone was to hurt you, then I'd kill them." She sighed as she pulled me back into her arms. "You know what's funny?" She quickly moved back to look at my face.

"What?" I sniffed.

"I'm not sure if my eyes are playing tricks, but..." Her voice trailed off as she tilted her head to one side.

"But?"

"But, it looks like it's changing." She pointed to my birthmark. "I can't decide if it's shrinking or fading or if I need glasses." She laughed. I laughed too, I didn't want to tell her it was both and why. "Have you not noticed?"

"I can't say that I have." I lied. I hated lying, especially to my sister, who I thought of as my best friend.

"Must be my eyes then." She laughed, but she didn't look convinced.

"Hey." The sound of someone else's voice broke her stare.

"Oh hi Jac.... Sean." She quickly looked back to me with an apologetic smile.

"Hi." I beamed as I stood up and went to walk towards him.

"Your Mum let me in." He pointed back into the house, and then turned to pull me into his arms.

He was sweaty and still wearing his football kit, which I had to say was making my heart go crazy. He looked so, well so sexy.

He was about to kiss me when he paused to look at me quizzically.

"Are you okay?" He asked concerned. I quickly nodded "You look like you've been crying." He stroked my face, like he was searching for traces of tears.

"Hay-fever." Kasey-Ray piped, to my relief.

"Oh, okay." His face relaxed as he finally leaned down to kiss me. "I missed you." He smiled as we came up for air. Then he quickly stepped away, making me wonder if I'd done something wrong. "Sorry." He quickly looked down at my clothes. I followed his gaze and realised my clothes were wet. "I forgot how sweaty I am."

"No, it's okay." I felt embarrassed on his behalf. I hadn't even noticed I was wet. "I'll quickly go get changed." I reached up and kissed him again. If I was already wet I may as well do it in style.

It was Kasey-Ray's coughing that made me realise we weren't alone.

"Sorry." It was my turn to apologise, as my face turned a deep shade of red. "Be back in a mo." I ran off, leaving Sean with my sister, jumping over the hoover wire as I went.

Before I'd gotten to my room, I'd managed to take off my clothes. I had no idea what I was going to wear as I threw my clothes into the washing basket and went to rummage through my drawers.

After five minutes I still hadn't found anything to wear, so I decided to go into Kasey-Ray's room. She was more fashion conscious than me, and had a lot more clothes, and of course it didn't take me long to find a purple, strappy, ankle length dress.

I quickly put it on and checked myself in Kasey-Ray's mirror. Before I left, I could hear voices coming from the back garden, so I decided to eavesdrop through my sisters opened bedroom window.

"I'm just warning you." I heard Kasey-Ray's stern voice. "If you hurt her, I'll kill you." I could hear the faint laugh from Sean in response. "It's not funny. She's never had a boyfriend or gotten close to anyone before, and I don't want you treating her like a toy that you can throw away when you're bored."

My heart was in my mouth. I felt sick. I had no idea how or why she was speaking to him like this. Had he said or done something when I'd left?

"Kasey-Ray?" Sean's calm voice spoke.

"Yes?" She huffed.

"I actually really love your sister and would never dream of hurting her."

"You better not." She cut in.

"Look, I've never felt like this about anyone before. If anyone is going to get hurt it would be me."

There was silence then. I had no idea what was going on. Why would he get hurt? My sister must have had the same confusion on her face as Sean spoke again.

"I worry that Erin will get bored of me and won't want me. I worry that she'll never feel for me the way I feel for her."

I crouched down low on the floor, unsure if I'd heard what I'd just heard.

"Erin? What are you doing in your sister's room?" My Mum's loud voice boomed, making me cringe as I put my finger to my lips. I was sure Sean and Kasey-Ray had heard her.

"I was looking for something to wear." I barely gasped.

God, how was I supposed to go down stairs and face him now? Surely they must know I was eavesdropping.

My Mum looked confused as I pointed to the open window and the realisation quickly covered her face.

"Sorry." She whispered. "But you shouldn't listen in on other peoples conversations anyway."

She said as an afterthought, but grabbing my arm as I tried to walk past. "Everything okay though?" She asked concerned.

"Yeah, just Kasey-Ray warning Sean not to hurt me." My Mum laughed as I did too.

"He better watch out then." She joked, as she released my arm.

I forced a smile as I walked away and slowly headed down the stairs. Before heading outside, I took a deep breath and tried to compose myself, a fake smile plastered on my face.

"I hope you don't mind?" I smiled apologetically to my sister, as I pulled at the dress. "I couldn't find anything to wear."

"No, no, that's fine." She quickly and nervously told me, "It looks good on you." She gave me a once over. "I'm going to go phone Claire. See ya later." She quickly told me as she hurried past, leaving me timidly standing there.

"You look good." Sean warmly smiled. "I won't hug you 'til I've showered." He laughed. "Don't want your Mum giving you another row for raiding your sister's drawers." I blushed. He had heard. I hoped he hadn't realised I was eavesdropping. "Shall we?"

He pointed towards the back door and I nodded as I led the way back into the house, towards the front door.

"Mum?" I called. "I'm going out."

My Mum appeared at the top of the stairs.

"Will you be back for dinner?"

"No, she's having dinner at mine with my family." Sean told her. This was news to me.

"Okay, be back by ten." She turned back to where she'd come from.

"I hope you don't mind." Sean said as he opened the front door for me.

"No." I forced another smile. I was nervous as I walked towards his car.

"My Dad's promised to be on his best behaviour." Even though he said this, he didn't look like he actually believed it.

We sat in silence for the ten minute journey. Every so often he would reach over and stroke my leg, sending tingles up and down my body.

When we pulled up outside his house, we sat there for a few minutes, still neither of us saying a word. It was Sean who finally broke the silence, when he turned to look at me.

"You heard what I said, didn't you?" I froze in my seat, not wanting to look at him or speak. I finally nodded. "I meant every word of it." He sat there staring as I finally turned to look at him. He sighed as he realised I didn't really believe him.

Don't get me wrong, I wanted to believe him, I really did, but I could never see how I could ever hurt him. Surely it was the other way round.

"You know I love you though, right?"

This I did believe, even though I didn't know why he did.

"Yes." I nodded. "I love you too."

This made him look relieved.

"I can live with that." He reached over to stroke my face. Then he gently leaned forward to kiss me. "Come on, let's get inside." He quickly got out of the car, and walked by my side as we went into the house. "I'm just going to take a shower. Make yourself at home."

Before I could respond, he was gone, leaving me standing there, in the living room. I wasn't alone though, as I spotted Kelly, Paul and James. They seemed to be glued at the hips.

"Hi Erin." Kelly smiled as she waved me over. "Come join us." I slowly walked over to sit down next to James, or was it Paul?

"Hi." I shyly spoke, as whomever I was sat next to me smiled.

The three of them were sat around a coffee table, with what looked like a giant map.

"What's that?" I asked as I leaned closer to get a better look.

"We're looking for Wally!" One of the twins laughed, not looking up from the map.

"Do you want to try and find him?" The twin sitting next to me asked with a playful smile.

"Sure." I kneeled down to get a closer look.

It wasn't a map, it was a giant cartoon picture of the seaside, with hundreds of people dressed in brightly coloured clothes.

"We're looking for this guy." Kelly pointed to a picture of a man wearing a red and white striped top, red hat and black glasses. I nodded, as I looked back down to the bigger picture. This was going to be hard, as nearly everyone was wearing similar clothing and glasses.

It took me about five minutes, when I spotted him Kelly cheered.

"We've been at this for nearly an hour." One of the twins laughed.

"You want to try another?" Kelly asked, as she rolled up the picture and pulled out another, this one was of a pirate ship.

"Sure." I smiled, happy to be part of a group who didn't seem to judge me, and seemed happy to be in my company.

This time it took me a little longer, but still I was the first to find Wally.

"Have you done this before?" The twin sitting next to me raised an eyebrow.

"No never." I never had, well not giant pictures like this. I had taken a 'Where's Wally?' book from the library when I was younger and ended up taking it back, without even looking at it.

He sat there looking serious, then sensing my unease, smiled and raised his hand for a high five, which I responded to.

"Third time lucky?" His brother asked. I nodded as Kelly pulled out another picture.

"Wow! You have a lot of these don't you?" I laughed.

"James's thing." Kelly pointed to the twin sitting next to me, which made me smile. I had been right. Maybe Kelly wasn't the only one who could tell them apart. But saying that, she never seemed to think about it. Telling them apart came naturally to her.

By the time I'd found Wally, for the third time, Sean appeared.

"Hey." he came and sat next to me, with a kiss.

"Hey." I smiled, as I leaned into him.

"Your girlfriend has sharp eyes." Paul winked at me. I smiled happily, more at the fact at hearing the word girlfriend. "Either that or she's cheating." he laughed.

"I found Wally three times." I boasted, proud of myself. "And no cheating involved." I put my tongue out at Paul.

"Well done." Sean kissed me again, and for a moment, I forgot we weren't alone.

"I think I'll have to go buy some more." I heard one of the twins say, as I pulled away from Sean. It was James and he actually looked excited at the prospect of buying more of these pictures.

"Make sure you get hard ones next time." I teased, making everyone laugh and James act offended.

"I'm going to see how my Mum's getting on in the kitchen." Sean whispered in my ear. "You coming?" I smiled and nodded, as Sean helped me up.

"Hey, where are you taking Erin?" Kelly asked in an unhappy tone.

"To the kitchen. Is that okay with you?" Sean teased.

Kelly laughed and nodded.

"Bring her back when you're done though." She ordered, as Sean walked backwards, with me in his arms.

"She's all mine." He told his sister, as he held me tightly and kissed my neck.

"You can't keep her to yourself ya know." Kelly scolded "Erin's my little sister now."

I slowly turned around, as Sean playfully held me tight, to see Kelly sticking her tongue out at Sean.

"You can share me." I laughed, as Sean playfully blew a raspberry on my neck, making me laugh.

"Nope, you're all mine." he turned me around, as he continued to walk backwards into the kitchen, as I waved bye.

"Oh, hi Erin." I heard Sean's Mum say, making me turn in the direction of her voice.

"Hi Ruth." I smiled, still in the tight hold of Sean. "Do you need any help?" I politely asked, but she shook her head.

"No. I'm pretty much done in here. Dinner will be ready in a couple of hours."

She seemed to have everything organised, as I looked around the kitchen to see pots of vegetables, sitting on the stove, ready to be switched on.

"How long have you been here?" She asked, as she looked at the clock on the wall.

"I'm not sure." I laughed, looking to Sean for an answer.

"About an hour. She's been playing 'Where's Wally?' with Kelly and the twins." He pointed towards the living room, as he released me and walked towards the cupboard to pull out two glasses and raised them towards me.

"Yes please."

"I hope they went easy on you." His Mum said as she turned to wipe down the sides.

"She showed them a thing or two." Sean laughed as he pulled out a carton of fresh orange juice and held it up as I nodded.

"Three to be exact." I laughed.

"I hope you don't mind." His Mum looked back towards the clock. "But I need to pop back to the gym and collect Sean's Dad."

"No, that's fine." I smiled, as she walked towards the kitchen door, patting my shoulder on the way out.

"Here." Sean handed me a glass of orange juice, as he walked past me and into the conservatory, where I followed.

Stepping into the conservatory, I gasped when I took in the full view of the back garden. I thought it was big the last time I was here, but seeing it from here was so surreal. I don't think I'd ever seen a garden this big.

Along one side was a high hedge, about 7 feet high, separating their garden and next. At the far end of the garden, there seemed to be a tennis court.

"Wow!" I gasped, as I went to sit down next to Sean on a two-seater wicker sofa with floral cushioned seats.

Sean followed my gaze, as he took my glass from my hands and placed it on a small table. Without a word, he stood up and took my hand and led me out of the conservatories side door.

It was all so breathtaking. There was a paved area, when I first stepped out, decorated with statues and a small fountain in the middle. To one side there was a path that led to the bottom of the garden, with brightly coloured flowers on either side.

We stopped for a while to look at the tennis court, which I reckoned was used frequently.

"Do you play?" I asked, without looking at him.

"Yep. My Mum is really good at it and often teaches people at weekends."

"Wow!"

Every day I felt like I learnt something knew about Sean and his family. No matter how much I tried to prepare myself, he always surprised me.

One thing I really liked was the fact he never shoved it in my face. He was very modest, and until I came to his house, I would never have guessed that his family had so much money.

"I want to show you something."

He led me back the way we came to another path that I'd seen half way down, which was lined with tall blossom trees. After about 50 metres, we came to what I thought was a small wooden house, about the size of an average bungalow.

Sean pulled a key from his pocket and unlocked the door.

"This is the summer house." Sean told me as he opened the door and we stepped into a room which held a large plasma TV on the wall, with every type of games console neatly placed in a stand underneath.

Next to this were stands full of console games. In one corner stood a stereo system, and next to it stood two old arcade machines, Pac man and Street Fighter.

In the middle was a large three-seater sofa, which looked more like a four seater. On the floor were five beanbags that were scattered about the room.

Whilst I looked around the room, Sean started opening the windows. I noticed there were several doors leading from this room.

"May I?" I pointed to the two doors at the back

of the room.

"Sure." Sean nodded, as he followed me into a small room, which held a fridge, microwave, and a couple of cupboards.

He walked past me to open the window as I went to look in the next, which was a small bathroom with a toilet, sink, shower and a bathroom cabinet.

As I closed the door behind me, I saw Sean entering another room, to the right of the bathroom. It was an average sized bedroom, with a double bed, wardrobe, TV and a two chest of drawers.

"This is my room, or whoever's if we have guests." He laughed. "And this." He led me to the next room. He laughed again when he saw my reaction. "This is the Jacuzzi room."

"Wow!"

There stood in the middle of the room was a large circular Jacuzzi that could probably fit about ten people.

"Do you use it?" I asked when I noticed it was empty.

"Yeah, we've just not used it in a couple of weeks." He walked over to open the windows. "You'll have to bring a swimsuit over next time." I blushed without answering him. "Let me show you the other two rooms."

He led me across the main room, to the two doors on the other side. The first door was another bedroom, set up the same way as the other bedroom.

"Kelly's." He nodded, closing the door behind him, and then walking through the next door, into the last room. This room held a pool table in the middle and a darts boards on one wall. "Fancy a quick game?"

He pointed at the pool table. I nodded with a smile. I wasn't very sporty, but one thing I knew I was good at, was pool.

"You can break." I smiled as I went to get a cue and apply some chalk. "And don't go easy on me 'cos I'm a girl." I joked with a wink.

"Oooooh, are you a pool shark?" He laughed, as he walked round to take the break shot.

"No, but I know how to play." I gave him an innocent smile, and it didn't take me long to show him how good I was.

"Oh, I'm going to have some fun with the others." He laughed as I looked at him, confused for a moment. "Justin is a bit of a pool shark, and Paul's pretty good too, but I don't think they have anything on you." I laughed as I went to put the cue back. "Let's keep this a secret for now. I want to see the look on their faces when you destroy them." I was nervous at this idea.

"I'm not that good."

"I beg to differ." He leant against the pool table and pulled me close. "Any other hidden talents I should know about?"

"Not that I am aware." I smiled.

"I bet you have." He winked as he pulled me closer for a kiss. "Let's head back and get our drinks." He said, standing up and taking my hand.

"Don't you need to close the windows?"

"Nah, Kelly and the twins will be down after dinner."

"Okay." I followed him out as he locked the door behind us before turning to take my hand.

"After we've gotten Dr Hammersmith out of the way tomorrow, we can come back here if you like?" I nodded nervously, as I remembered about Dr Hammersmith. I had no idea what tests he wanted to do, and I felt too sick and nervous to ask if Sean knew. I just nodded as he continued to talk.

"My Poppa and Gran would like to meet you. Are you okay with that?" He watched my face for a reaction.

"I would love to." I smiled, and I meant it. "I have a few questions I would like to ask them."

"Poppa would love that." He gently squeezed my hand, and with a smile he leant across to kiss my cheek.

Chapter 12

By the time we'd gotten back to the house, Sean's parents were back. Sean had taken my glass and went to put ice cubes in it as I hovered at the kitchen door.

"Erin." Sean's Dad, Brian, crossed the room to hug me and kiss my cheek. "How are you?"

"Good thanks." I smiled shyly.

"You're looking lovely." He smiled as he looked me up and down, making me blush.

"Thanks. This is my sister's." I cringed. Why did I have to tell him I was wearing my sister's clothes? I think 'thanks' would have been enough.

"Here you go." Sean came to stand protectively, next to me, as he handed me my glass of orange juice.

"Thanks." I smiled.

"I hope my son's looking after you?" Brian raised an eyebrow at Sean.

"Most definitely." I flustered.

"Of course, Dad." Sean dryly told him.

"Dinner will be ready in about fifteen minutes." Ruth called, breaking the friction.

"We'll be in the conservatory."

"What's the deal with you and your Dad?" I whispered as we sat down.

"Nothing really." He shrugged.

"Nothing really?" I raised an eyebrow. He sighed when he realised I wasn't going to let this go.

"Firstly, he isn't happy that I'm not as into sports as I was."

"And?" I knew there was more and I would drag it out of him, if I had to.

"I still don't like the way he spoke to you, the first time you met him." He held his hand up before I spoke. "And he wants me to follow in his footsteps and manage the gym, or the other one he plans on opening, and I still don't know if that's what I want to do." He sighed.

"Firstly, your Dad is fine with me, so don't worry about that." I cuddled up next to him, and we stayed like that for a few minutes, neither of us speaking, then I quickly sat up and turned to look at him.

"What do you enjoy doing?" I asked, intrigued.

"Besides spending time with you?" He laughed. I nodded in reply. "I really do enjoy kickboxing." He told me thoughtfully. "I would actually like to teach people." He seemed to light up at this thought.

"Why don't you then?" He paused for a moment as he thought it over.

"Hmmm..." He smiled. "I like the sound of that."

"Maybe you could use one of the rooms at the gym." He seemed to think about this, then all of a sudden he kissed me and gave me a huge hug.

"I love it, and I love you." He kissed me again. I laughed at seeing him so excited.

"Dinner's ready." Kelly called.

We got up and Sean took my hand and led me to a chair in the kitchen, next to his. He looked like he was ready to burst, as everyone sat down.

"Dad?" Sean spoke like an over-excited child. "How would you feel if I used one of the halls at the gym to teach kickboxing?"

The whole table fell silent as eyes moved between Sean and Brian.

"I think it's an excellent idea." Ruth finally spoke, breaking the silence.

Sean smiled enthusiastically as he stroked my cheek.

"It was Erin's idea." This seemed to break whatever thoughts Brian was thinking.

"Was it really?" Brian asked, as I nervously fidgeted in my seat, making Sean place his hand to my left cheek and stroke my birthmark.

"Kind of..." My throat was dry as I spoke.

"I really like it." Brian smiled as I sighed with relief. James, who was sat next to me, patted my back. Then Brian turned to look at Sean. "We'll

~ 264 ~

need to sort out a business plan and discuss advertising."

They continued talking as I saw Ruth mouth the words, 'Thank you.'

For the rest of the meal, Sean and Brian happily discussed all the details, leaving everyone else hardly getting a word in edgeways. Even when we had all finished, Sean and his Dad stayed at the table talking as I helped Ruth clear up.

"Thanks for that." Ruth pointed to her son and husband. "It's been a while since I've seen them have a proper conversation, without a fight nearly breaking out." She looked happy and relieved as I handed her dishes to put in the dishwasher. "How did you come up with it?" She asked puzzled. "Brian's been on at him for months to decide what he wants to do."

"I just asked him what he enjoys." I shrugged. Ruth looked at me and started laughing.

"I think that's the one thing no one asked him." She closed the dishwasher then turned it on. "Are you going to be one of his students?" She asked seriously. It was my turn to laugh.

"I don't think so."

"Why not?" She picked up a cloth and a bottle of disinfectant and started cleaning the sides.

"Not my cup of tea." I laughed.

"I know what you mean." Ruth smiled with a wink.

"Erin?" Kelly called from the conservatory door.

"Yes?" I turned to look at her.

"We're off to the summer house." She pointed in the direction of it. "You fancy coming?" I looked at Sean, who had looked up at me.

"Go ahead. I'll follow down in a bit." I leaned down to give him a kiss as I walked over to follow Kelly and the twins. I paused at the doorway to look at Ruth.

"You don't need any help do you?"

"Not at all. You go ahead and have fun." She smiled.

Smiling back, I followed Kelly into the garden.

"Have you been to the summerhouse before?" She asked as we walked side by side, as the twins ran ahead.

"Yeah, Sean gave me a tour before dinner."

We carried on walking in silence. I was unsure what to say. I wasn't used to being around people and I'd never had a proper conversation with Kelly before.

"I was thinking of going clothes shopping at the end of the month, do you fancy coming?" She breezily asked me.

"Sure." I smiled, and she seemed to sigh with relief.

"I normally go alone. Paul and James aren't really into shopping, unless it's for themselves and my Mum is always working." I nodded as I listened. "I don't actually relate well to other girls since all of this, and most people don't understand what's going on with me and the twins." She said with a sad sigh.

"I never seem to relate to anyone full stop" I laughed nervously. Kelly gave me a warm smile in reply.

"Well, I hope that will change now." She gently touched my shoulder. "And thanks."

"What for?" I asked confused.

"Sean and my Dad, and for making my brother happy. It's been a long time since I've seen him so happy." She paused and looked at me. "Actually, I don't think I've ever seen him this happy before, so thank you." She gave me a wide genuine smile.

"You're welcome?" I laughed more in confusion as to whether they were the right words.

By the time the summerhouse came into view the twins were already inside.

"I actually expected you to have lots of friends." I had heard that Kelly was popular, like Kasey-Ray.

"I did." We entered the summerhouse to find the twins sitting on two beanbags with one of the games consoles switched on. "But when I found out what I could do, I found it hard to talk to others, I was actually nervous in case I revealed myself in front of my friends." She went to sit in front of the sofa, kicking her shoes off and pulling her feet up.

"Eventually my friends stopped calling." She shrugged and actually seemed upset thinking about it. Sensing this, the twins moved in unison, towards Kelly and rested their heads on her legs. There was something so comforting and loving as I watched the three of them. "On a plus though." She smiled as she leaned down and gave each twin a kiss on the head. "I have met these two." She looked so happy as she spoke about them.

"How did you get together?" I enquired.

They were fascinating and I wanted to know everything, but I didn't know them all that well, so I didn't expect Kelly to fill me in on all of it, just yet.

"Well, it was through Sean. He had started hanging around with them, and they were always round here. I couldn't get rid of them if I tried." She teased, making the twins quickly look up, with faces like they were offended. "Was funny though. They seemed to hate each other." The twins laughed at this. "I knew I had feelings for them, but I had no idea which. I actually thought it was because they were so identical, that I couldn't tell them apart, well not at first." She smiled. "But I soon found out that they were complete opposites, and I love them both equally."

She paused to look at Paul and James, lovingly. Then quickly turned and leaned over to touch my leg, with a laugh.

"You know what's funny?" I shook my head. "The day we got together was the day they stopped arguing. Their family love me for that. They still find our relationship weird, but love the fact I've brought them together." She laughed as me and the twins joined in.

"What's so funny?" Sean asked, as he came to sit next to me on the sofa.

"I was just telling Erin about how these two used to fight before we got together."

"Ah, I remember so well." Sean laughed too as he leaned into me. I raised my arm as he rested his head on my lap. "They used to have proper fist fights, and there's no way they would be sitting there like that, playing a game together." He laughed.

"We weren't that bad." Paul scoffed.

"You were." Sean continued laughing. "I remember one time you two had a fight over a game of football and me and Justin had to separate you both."

Paul didn't reply to this as he turned back to the game he and James were playing, as I started to stroke Sean's hair.

"So?" Kelly playfully slapped Sean's leg.

Sean moved his knees to one side, so he could see his sister, and gave her a puzzled expression.

"What happened with you and Dad?" Sean smiled but said nothing. "Come one, don't keep us in suspense."

The twins paused the game they were playing and turned to look at Sean with interest.

"Okay, okay." He laughed, as he sat up, swapping seats with me so his back was against the armrest and his legs were bent over mine. "He seems really excited. I think more so that I'm excited about doing this and he said that if it takes off then we will kit one hall out for my classes. I just need to get certified as an instructor before we can do anything else." Everyone was nodding, I wasn't sure if they knew anything about kickboxing or the process, I knew I had no idea. "Luckily my sensei has a certification program and said I can start next week. I also have to get a police check and insurance."

"Oh well, that's you out then. The police will fail you." James laughed.

"Ha-ha." Sean playfully kicked his shoulder. "Anyway I'm really looking forward to it. Probably be a slow start, but I hope it takes off."

"Me too." I whispered, proud of him. He leaned over to kiss me.

"So who fancies a game of pool?" Sean went to stand up, as I looked at him like I was a deer in headlights.

Paul's laugh interrupted my panic.

"You wanting your arse handed to you again do you?" Paul stood up, putting his controller down. Sean laughed as he winked at me.

"How about a game of doubles? I'll have Erin and you choose whoever."

"Do you want me to play one handed, to give you a chance?" The more cocky Paul became, the more my nervousness calmed and I wanted to play and beat him. "Trust me, you will need both your arms." I teased, making everyone stop to look at me. I was surprised at my fighting talk. It didn't have the effect I wanted, as I think Paul thought I was hyping up my boyfriend.

"Have you seen Sean play?" Paul laughed as he pointed at Sean. I nodded as I followed them into the other room.

"But I think this game, he may show you a thing or two." I smiled as I picked up a cue. "You can break." I smiled sweetly at Paul, and for a second he looked nervous.

"Bruv?" He called to James, and then quickly looked at Kelly.

"Go ahead, I'll watch. I have a feeling this may be an interesting game." Kelly went to sit on one of the stools.

For the start of the game, Paul was laughing as he took his turn, then Sean, and then James. Eventually it was my turn and I managed to sink four balls, along with wiping the smile off Paul's face.

By the time Sean had finished his turn, both sides had one ball each and the black. James sank the last ball and was now on the black. He didn't manage to pot it, but lined me up perfectly to sink the last remaining ball.

As I got ready to take the final shot, I looked up at Paul and smiled.

"Any final words?" I heard Kelly and Sean laugh. I kept my eyes still on Paul as I took my shot and sank the black. Sean high fived me as I stood up straight and went to put the cue back.

Paul was still staring at the pool table, expressionless. We all turned to look at him. I was unsure of what he was thinking. Was he angry? Then he started laughing, as he turned to me and held out his hand.

"Well played." He said sincerely and then turned to look at Sean. "You could have told me that you had a hustler as a girlfriend." Sean laughed.

"And miss seeing the look on your face? I don't think so." Sean came to stand behind me, pulling me into his arms as his cheek pressed against mine.

"Oh, you have to play Justin." Paul quickly said as he rubbed his hands together at this thought.

"Where is Justin?" I asked, stopping the laughter dead.

"He hasn't forgiven himself over what Jessica did to you." James quietly spoke.

The sound of Jessica's name made me flinch. Sean kissed my cheek as he gave me a gentle squeeze.

No one said anything, and it felt like we had stood there for ten minutes before Sean finally spoke.

"Anyway, I want some time alone with my pretty lady, before I take her home." He lightly stepped to my side as he kept one arm around me. "See you guys later."

"Bye." I waved as Sean led me out of the summerhouse, leaving Kelly, Paul and James standing there, silently watching us leave.

"What do you fancy doing?" Sean moved his hand from my waist to hold my hand.

"I don't know." I shrugged. I'd lost the will to do anything after Jessica's name was mentioned. "I'm actually feeling really tired."

Sean stopped suddenly, almost dragging me backwards, because he was still holding my hand.

"What's wrong? Are you okay?" He asked me, pulling me in front of him.

"Yeah I'm fine. Just tired." I faked a yawn.

"Did that upset you?" He pointed back to where we had just come from.

"No, not at all." I lied, hoping I sounded convincing. "I'm just really tired and I want to be wide awake for seeing Dr Hammersmith tomorrow."

"Hmmm..." he didn't look convinced as he still stood there looking at me.

Eventually he sighed and started walking.

"Okay." He didn't look like he believed a word I'd said, but I was relieved when he didn't press me further.

We carried on walking in silence. The only time we spoke was when we got inside his house.

"I'm just going to take Erin home." Sean told his parents, who were sat watching TV.

"Okay, bye love and I'll see you soon." Ruth lifted her hand to touch my arm.

"Bye Erin." Brian smiled.

I waved as I followed Sean outside and climbed into the car.

For the whole ten minute journey, neither of us spoke. Finally when we pulled up outside the house Sean switched off the engine and turned to look at me as he reached over to touch my face.

"You okay?" He seemed really concerned now as I turned to look at him.

"Yeah I'm fine. Honest." I forced a huge smile. "I'll see you in the morning"

Then I leaned over to kiss him, which took him by surprise at first, as it was always him who made the first move, but he didn't complain.

"I love you." He whispered as we eventually pulled away.

"I love you too." I smiled, leaning in for one more quick kiss, and then turned to get out of the car.

"I'll be round about nine." He told me when I had walked round to the driver's side of his car. "I'll text you when I'm leaving."

"Okay." I stole another kiss, and turned to head inside. "Night." I called after him as he started his engine and eventually pulled away as I went inside.

Chapter 13

The day had come to finally go and see Dr Hammersmith. I was nervous as we turned into the long drive.

Up ahead stood a very old mansion. I wasn't sure if the word mansion was fitting either. House was too small a word. This place was grand and well looked after. It seemed to have been standing there for hundreds of years. Ivy clung to the walls like it was holding on for dear life.

The main doors were securely locked and Sean held our ID cards up to a small camera, after a few moments we were buzzed in.

The inside of the building was completely different from the outside. It looked odd in comparison. The corridors were long and white, like a hospital.

There was no one about as we walked to the end of the corridor to a lift with big black doors. All the way it felt like a million eyes were on me. It didn't help that every few steps a camera would whirr and follow us.

Once inside the lift Sean pressed the button for the third floor, all the time not saying a word.

When the doors opened, we were greeted by a very elegant and attractive woman, who looked to be in her late twenties. She wore a navy blue suit and her hair was tied neatly into a twist at the back of her head.

"Sean." She purred, as we stepped out of the lift. "If you would like to follow me, Dr Hammersmith is waiting for you both." She eyed me critically, then turned her attention back to Sean, as we continued to walk down another long corridor.

Half way down she knocked on one of the side doors. After we heard Dr Hammersmith invite us in, she opened the door.

"Erin. Sean!" He beamed at us both. "Please take a seat." He gestured to two armchairs, in front of a large teak table and nodded at the woman as she quietly left, closing the door behind her.

The room looked like any other doctors office I had visited and you could smell the cleanliness in the air.

We sat down in the two chairs as Dr Hammersmith went to sit behind his desk, and pulled out a medical folder.

"Firstly, I would like to start by taking a few small tests, such as height, weight, blood pressure, so on and so forth, before we move onto the final test."

I looked at Sean, nervously, as he held my hand. We still hadn't spoken since we had entered the building and he looked like he was concentrating on the doctor.

The tests were like any other medical. I'd had one earlier in the year, when I moved to Galladale. The only difference was he asked to take my temperature, telling me that he would need to take it again, after the final test.

After he put the thermometer away, Dr Hammersmith turned to look at me. With a slight hesitation, he sat down and gave me a long hard look.

"I'm sure by now that Sean has been filling you in on different people and their powers?" Raising his eyebrows as he looked from myself to Sean then back to me.

"Well I know about my parents." It may have taken me 14 years but I knew about them now, and they didn't half know how to keep it a secret. I hoped I could learn from them. "Sean has also told me about his sister and the twins." I counted each name off on my fingers. "Oh and Justin."

Whilst I had been talking the doctor had started making notes of everything I was saying. Well I think that was what he was doing. It was a bit unnerving as I had no idea why he was doing it, and wasn't it just plain rude to write whilst someone is talking to you?

This last bit of information I gave, seemed to intrigue him, because he actually stopped writing and looked up at me with a huge smile on his face.

"Really? Oh please enlighten me."

Was he mocking me? He was even laughing as I looked nervously at Sean, who wouldn't even look at me. "He's a trainer?" I tried to sound confident.

That's what Sean had told me, but now I was getting the distinct impression I was wrong. Especially since Sean wasn't bothering to help me out.

"Yes, he is a trainer." I sighed as he said this. "Of sorts" Of sorts? What the heck did he mean by that? "He can make people do what he says."

He wrote something else down in his notepad. Tore it off. Then put it in a folder, before closing it.

It felt like an eternity before he spoke again. I wasn't sure what he meant. How could Justin make people do whatever he wanted them to do?

"I know pretty much what goes on in Galladale. I also know who has powers, even before they know themselves." He smiled at me thoughtfully. It was like he was trying to decide whether to continue or not.

His gaze turned towards Sean, who was still avoiding eye contact. This was making me feel very uneasy. I felt nausea sweeping over me. I probably would have started crying if the doctor hadn't started talking again. All I was thinking about was why wasn't Sean saying anything? I thought he loved me.

"I knew you had powers the day you were born."

Okay, this startled me. It was sending me on a whole different train of thought. How the heck could he have known when my own parents were unsure? Plus my parents had never mentioned that they were friends with him. I wasn't even born round here. So he wouldn't have seen me.

"When you moved here, I knew you had no idea. And I knew you needed a little bit of coaxing. So I asked Justin to train someone to bring out your fiery side." He said this like it was something you do every day. He was even laughing. Mind you he was the only one. "I knew what you were and I knew who your soul mate was." He really looked like he was enjoying himself. All he needed now was to look like a haggard old witch and stir a large cauldron. His cackle was perfect for it.

"Well to cut a long story short." He winked as slapped his thigh. "I got Justin to get Jessica to attack you. And Sean to provoke her by continuing to go near you."

He roared with laughter. He even touched my leg as a hint to join in with the laughter. I wasn't laughing. I didn't find any of it funny in the slightest. Right now I wanted to rip him to pieces. I wanted to see who would be laughing after I rammed his pencil in his eye.

Suddenly I jumped as I realised Sean was stroking my arm. Did he know all of this? Did he find it funny?

He doesn't love me. He never did. This was all some act. Some ploy to get me here so they could humiliate me. I wanted run away. Far, far away. Maybe another country.

I stood up ready to leave.

"Oh yes we have one more test."

"I'm going home." I spat. I was not putting up with any more of his rubbish.

"I don't think so." The doctor shook his head. Laughter leaving his face. "You are allowed to go after the last test." He turned to the boy I thought loved me. He nodded from Sean to me. "Please escort the lovely Erin next door."

Oh my God. Was Sean actually going to do what he said?

"Sean?" I pleaded, as I tried to make eye contact.

Finally he raised his eyes to mine. I couldn't make out what was going on in his head.

"Please." He barely whispered. "Then we can go home."

He had to be joking right? He hadn't spoken to me since we got here. He's been hiding the truth from me. Was he expecting me to start gushing and say, 'Oh sure baby, anything for you.' I knew it was too good to be true. He was too good to be true.

But, and this was a big but, if I go and do this last test, I could go home, then I wouldn't have to bother with him again. I'd go back to my normal life. The life I had before him. My lonely life, where no one spoke to me.

With a heavy sigh I nodded.

I still wasn't sure what the final test was, as we all went to go into another room.

The next room was the size of a gym hall, but with a glass room at one end. Everything was pristine white. I was led to the centre of the room and told to wait there for further instructions, as Dr Hammersmith and Sean went into the small glass room, where the woman, we'd met earlier and a small balding man in a lab coat, were sitting.

I had no idea what was going on. I was scared and stared helplessly at Sean, whose expression seemed pained. He couldn't look me in the eye.

Then there was a sound of a door opening and closing, from behind me. Seeing the alarm in Sean's eyes, I turned to look behind me and standing there, looking as scared as me, was Jessica. A look of confusion crossing both of our faces.

I looked back to the glass room to see Sean arguing with Dr Hammersmith. I couldn't hear what was being said. I turned slowly back to Jessica, who by now was looking petrified.

Dr Hammersmith's voice boomed through the Tannoy system, making us both jump.

"Here is your chance to get your revenge."

The statement made Jessica start to cry hysterically. I was frightened. What did they expect me to do? I wasn't a fighter? I didn't want to hurt Jessica.

In a split second, Jessica was on her knees, gripping tightly to my wrists, begging for forgiveness. But I didn't hear what she was saying. The rage came from nowhere. All I saw was red. I looked down at her, with hate filled eyes, as the flames blazed from my body, licking at Jessica's.

She didn't release her hands and I couldn't hear her blood curdling scream's, as Sean tried to break me from my trance.

It was the sound like Velcro ripping that snapped me out of it. I stood there, motionless, as Jessica's scream echoed around the room, from her blistered body. Her hair was singed and the smell of burnt flesh stung the back of my throat.

Someone was pouring water over her. The sound of the water hissed as it touched her charred skin, and steam floated up.

Then everything went black.

Chapter 14

It was dark when my screams woke me up. I was in my own bed and it was soaked from my sweat. I knew the nightmare I'd had was true when I looked into Sean's eyes, who was sat in a chair next to my bed, as he leant over to stroke my face.

I turned away from his hurt filled eyes and lay back down, with my back to him.

"Why didn't you stop me?" I whispered in the dark, as tears rolled from my eyes and onto my pillow. I tried to block the images of Jessica lying there burnt. Burnt by me. I was still a monster, just worse than the ugly one I use to think of myself.

"I tried." He sounded like he'd been crying too.

"Not hard enough." I snapped as I sat up to push his hands off me. He didn't argue. He just sat there, looking at the floor. I refused to acknowledge the sadness and guilt that sat there in his eyes. "Is she still alive?" He nodded, as I barely managed to ask that question. "I could have killed her."

Sean didn't respond. He just sat there in silence, staring at his hands as he fidgeted restlessly. I still couldn't shake the horrific images.

"I think you should go." I whispered. I didn't want him to go, but I felt something inside me pushing him away. How could I be with someone who could watch me torture someone so inexcusably?

He reached out to me in the dark, but I moved back just out of his reach. I could see the pain I was causing him and it tore at my heart as I watched him walk out of my bedroom.

***

The next week passed in a blur. I spent most of my time in my bedroom, leaving only to go to the bathroom. I was vaguely aware it was raining and had been the whole week. Not that I'd looked out of the window, it was Kasey-Ray's cries, every morning when she got up.

Sean had tried to see me several times and called me constantly, but I refused to see or speak to him. I could see it starting to grate on my parents and how they hated explaining to Sean that I wouldn't come to the phone or door.

By the second week, my parents had had enough. I'd heard my Mum and Kasey-Ray leave to go and do the weekly shopping. Usually it would be both my parents, who would go, and Kasey-Ray would have been out gallivanting somewhere with her friends, but with all this rain, there wasn't much to do. I'd heard her moan about it being the summer holidays and where in the summer should it rain all the time. I knew it was Sean causing the rain, whether consciously or not.

I heard my parent's car pulling out of the drive, just as my bedroom door opened.

"This has to stop." My Dad rumbled as the room started to shake.

"You don't understand." I sighed unhappily.

My Dad's face turned red and what felt like the whole house, started to shake.

"Don't you dare say I don't understand." He took the four steps from my bedroom door to my bed, where I lay, in less than a second. "Don't you dare blame that poor boy for Dr Hammersmith's experiments."

This infuriated me. How could he defend him? Flames started to build. Ignoring this, my Dad continued.

"If Sean had his way, you wouldn't have even gone for that final test." He looked at me, carefully judging my mood, as he walked to the chair at my desk. Sighing he sat down.

"Dr Hammersmith is not someone you disobey. I know I've tried." He frowned sadly, as if he were remembering something. "He uses trainers, like Justin, to control weak minded people." He paused to look at me, "Like Jessica. Dr Hammersmith chose her specifically to torment you. It broke

Justin's heart, as he'd became quite attached to her and deep down she was sweet hearted." He shook his head. "It's a shame you never saw that side of her."

"What exactly does a trainer do?" I asked, shocked by what I'd heard and curious at the same time.

"Depending on what Dr Hammersmith requires, he can bring out your best or worst trait." My Dad shrugged like he didn't completely understand it either.

"Did Sean know?" I felt I really needed to know this. If he had known all along then that would mean our relationship was fake and he'd used me.

I brushed the tears from my eyes as my Dad shook his head.

"Not at first, but that day at school, in the changing rooms." I looked at him with panic. My Dad held a hand up. "Yes we know about that, and that was when Sean found out and decided that even though Justin couldn't stop with his control over

Jessica, he could, however, stay away from you, so she wouldn't hurt you."

I sat and thought about this, as my Dad stood up from his seat and walked over to the window seat and sat down.

"He loves you sweetie and I know you love him. It hurts him being apart from you. Do you think Mother Nature is causing all this rain?" He waved his hand at the window and looked back to me thoughtfully, but I already knew the answer. "He tried to get him to stop." He whispered. "Dr Hammersmith I mean. They locked Sean in that room and made him watch. He feels your pain, I should know." He told me, as he buried his face in his hands.

"We were 12 years old when Dr Hammersmith tried a similar experiment on your mother. You know he never ages." He added thoughtfully, like he'd only just realised. "Well, unlike Jessica, this girl didn't survive." By now he was crying as he was remembering the horrific event. "You see, this girl had also been taught to attack your mother. Apparently this helps bring on our gifts. Your Mum couldn't control her rage and numerous lightning bolts struck the girl, where she stood. I was powerless."

I crossed the room to where he sat, hands still buried in his hands, as I knelt down at his feet. Sensing me there, he looked at me through his red rimmed eyes.

"It could have broken us both, if we weren't so strong. I couldn't have changed anything, even if I could turn back time." Sitting in silence, I listened to everything he'd said. "Please don't punish him more than he is hurting now." I turned to look at the clock, 2:38pm.

"Dad?" He looked at me with sad eyes. "I'm going out!" I quickly stood up and started to run down the stairs. "Don't make me any dinner."

"What about your coat?" My Dad called after me.

"Don't need one." I shouted.

***

I ran the thirty minute walk to his house, taking short cuts through different fields. I knew he got home around 3:15pm, and I wanted to be there before he did.

I got there with five minutes to spare and almost collapsed on the steps outside his house. I saw Kelly hesitate at one of the windows and decide to just leave me be.

I looked like a drowned rat, but I didn't care. I sat staring at the road searching for a glimpse of his car. When it appeared a little after 3:20pm, I stood up and waited for him to get out of the car.

At first he just sat staring at me through the windshield watching me nervously play with my hands.

Slowly he opened his car door and climbed out, closing the door, without looking at me. When he turned to face me, my stomach twisted into knots, as I looked at the sadness in his face. That's all I needed to make me rush over to him and throw my arms around him.

Cupping my hand around the back of his head, I pulled his head down to kiss his cheek. He didn't respond he just stood there looking down at the ground. I pulled his face to mine and looked up to his sad eyes. I wasn't sure if he was crying or it was the rain on his cheeks. We stood there, foreheads pressed together.

"Hey." I whispered as he finally relented and looked me in the eyes. "I love you." I stretched up to kiss him. The pain on his face was obvious and it showed when he kissed me back.

"I love you so much." He almost cried out.

By now we were both soaking wet and neither of us seemed to care.

"I'm so sorry." We both said at the same time, as he reached up to stroke my left cheek. I leaned into his hand, I had so missed him doing this.

"You've nothing to be sorry for." He started to say, as I moved my fingers to his lips and shushed him. When he tried to speak again, I reached up to kiss him, this time he kissed me back more urgently.

Eventually he pulled away and took a step back to examine me, with his hands holding my shoulders. By now the rain had stopped.

"Come on, let's get you inside." He pulled me to his side and we walked up the steps and into his house.

"Kelly?" Sean called as she appeared from the kitchen, glowering at me. "Can Erin borrow some of your clothes, whilst her clothes dry please?" She grunted and headed upstairs, where we followed her.

"I'll be in my room." He pointed to a door I assumed was his. "Just come through when you're finished."

I followed Kelly into her room and stood looking around at all the different purples and blues, she had in her room. I hadn't realised there were so many different shades.

Kelly shoved a pair of jeans and t-shirt in my hands, with force. I flinched and said nothing. I was sure she was going to give me a piece of her mind, and I wanted her to.

She disappeared for a minute and when she returned she launched a towel at me.

"Thanks." I smiled at her timidly.

"Look, don't thank me." She stepped closer to point a finger in my face. "You're lucky I don't beat the hell out of you." I laughed nervously, which seemed to irate her more. "This isn't a laughing matter." She hissed like she was a kettle. I expected steam to come out of her ears. I noticed her alarm clock switch off. "He's my brother and you have no idea how much he loves you and how much he's been hurting over you." She stepped away and went to punch the door, but stopped, thinking better of it. With her hand on the door, she turned to look at me. "But if you ever hurt him like that again, so help me, I'll..."

"Kelly!" I heard Sean shout from the other room, stopping her finishing off what she was saying. She grunted and looked at me, slightly calmer.

"I'm warning you, okay?"

I nodded as I heard Sean shout at his sister again. When she left I heard them arguing on the landing. I couldn't quite make out what was being said though. I didn't feel scared or angry. I deserved everything she dished out.

I started undressing and wrapped myself in the towel. Jesus, they're soaking. I could have probably wrung them out and filled a half-pint glass with water.

Once I got dressed and towel dried my hair, I picked up my clothes and towel and carried them to the room Sean had pointed to. I knocked before opening the door. Sean was putting a CD in his stereo and smiled as he saw me walking in.

"I hope you don't mind James Morrison?"

"No that's fine." I answered as he took the wet clothes and towel from me to hang on his radiator, as the song ''Under the influence'' started playing.

Sitting on his bed, I looked around his room. His room was blue and white, posters of his favourite football team hung on the walls. On one wall there were four shelves, three with CD's and one with books. On another wall there were at least ten shelves full of trophies, football, rugby, swimming, tennis and athletics. I even spotted some martial arts ones.

"Impressive." I pointed to them

"Yeah, not bad." He laughed as he climbed onto the bed behind me and lay down as I continued to sit there, looking around his room.

"You have a tidy up whilst I was getting changed?" I teased as I spotted a pile of clothes thrown into the corner.

"You caught me." He laughed as he raised his arms up, then reached over and pulled me down next to him.

I lay on my back, whilst he lay on his side, propped up on one arm, running his fingers over my body, sending waves of electricity over me.

"I missed you." He smiled as he watched my body dance where his fingers touched.

"I missed you too." I bit my lip trembling as tears filled my eyes.

I hadn't realised up until now how stupid I'd been. He must have felt my body freeze as he quickly looked up, eyes full of concern.

"What's wrong?" He put his hand to my cheek. "Did I do something wrong?" I shook my head. "Was it Kelly? I'll kill her." He shouted, without waiting for an answer, he tried to climb off the bed, but I stopped him, pulling him down on top of me to kiss him.

When I stopped, his eyes were confused and full of concern.

"I'm sorry." I whispered over choked tears. "I shouldn't have treated you like that..." I didn't manage to finish off what I was saying, because he was kissing me.

When he stopped, he went back to lying at the side of me, pulling me onto my side to face him.

"I don't want to ever hear you apologising." He held his hand up to stop me from talking. "You had every right to act the way you did."

"Shhhh..." I placed a finger to his lips. "I'll stop apologising." I saw him smiling. "If you don't apologise."

I left him to ponder this for a moment, and then he sighed and nodded.

***

The summer holiday seemed to fly by. I'd finally gotten around to telling Kasey-Ray about my gift, with Sean as back up, in case I did something stupid.

At first she was angry about being kept in the dark, and then her anger had turned to frustration, as she wondered what her gift would be. Then the frustration gave through to excitement. She was convinced that she had a gift. She spent the rest of the holiday in the garden, trying to get angry, in a hope it would show her gift.

She looked like a raving lunatic. We spent a lot of the time in the garden, laughing at her, mainly because she looked absolutely ridiculous and also in the hope it would make her angry and she would hopefully find her gift, if she had one, and stop acting like a mad woman.

She never did get angry though. She ended up sitting on the floor, laughing at herself.

Sean and I were rarely apart, except when he was at work and most nights. Some weekends my family and I would go to the cottage with Sean, sometimes the rest of them would come over.

But before we knew it, the holidays were over and it was time to go back to school.

Sean drove Kasey-Ray and I, and as soon as we pulled into the car park, Kasey-Ray quickly jumped out.

I was nervous as we sat there looking out of the window, Sean's hand stoking my leg.

I sighed as I pulled down the sun-visor to look in the mirror. I smiled as I looked at my birthmark, which was pretty much gone. I leaned over to kiss Sean.

"I'll see you at lunch." He told me again. We had decided to have a picnic at the place we had first met. "I love you." He purred as he gave me another kiss.

"I love you too."

Taking a deep breath, I opened the passenger door and stepped out to take my first day of my last year of high school.

With a huge smile on my face and a bounce in my step, I made my way to the school's main door, ignoring everyone's stares.

I knew now that they weren't staring at me because they were repulsed, and whatever their thoughts were now, I didn't care. To me, I was the happiest person on this planet and in love with the most wonderful and most beautiful man alive, and nothing could make me feel any different.

Could it?

Information

For more information on Erin the Fire Goddess check out my Facebook page:

https://www.facebook.com/ErinTheFireGoddess
http://amazon.com/author/laviniaurban
http://laviniaurban.co.uk
@ErinFireGoddess
@Lavinia_Missb

About Author

Lavinia originally grew up in Cheshire and now lives in a small village just outside of Edinburgh with her husband and two daughters.

Writing has always been something that Lavinia have loved since an early age but it wasn't until 2010 when the idea came to her to write Erin the Fire Goddess.

Lavinia chose to name the main character and her sister after her two daughters, who inspire Lavinia to write every day.